SUSAN SCA
MURDER WHILE YOU WORK

SUSAN Scarlett is a pseudonym of the author Noel Streatfeild (1895-1986). She was born in Sussex, England, the second of five surviving children of William Champion Streatfeild, later the Bishop of Lewes, and Janet Venn. As a child she showed an interest in acting, and upon reaching adulthood sought a career in theatre, which she pursued for ten years, in addition to modelling. Her familiarity with the stage was the basis for many of her popular books.

Her first children's book was *Ballet Shoes* (1936), which launched a successful career writing for children. In addition to children's books and memoirs, she also wrote fiction for adults, including romantic novels under the name 'Susan Scarlett'. The twelve Susan Scarlett novels are now republished by Dean Street Press.

Noel Streatfeild was appointed an Officer of the Order of the British Empire (OBE) in 1983.

ADULT FICTION BY NOEL STREATFEILD

As Noel Streatfeild

The Whicharts (1931)

Parson's Nine (1932)

Tops and Bottoms (1933)

A Shepherdess of Sheep (1934)

It Pays to be Good (1936)

Caroline England (1937)

Luke (1939)

The Winter is Past (1940)

I Ordered a Table for Six (1942)

Myra Carroll (1944)

Saplings (1945)

Grass in Piccadilly (1947)

Mothering Sunday (1950)

Aunt Clara (1952)

Judith (1956)

The Silent Speaker (1961)

As Susan Scarlett
(All available from Dean Street Press)

Clothes-Pegs (1939)

Sally-Ann (1939)

Peter and Paul (1940)

Ten Way Street (1940)

The Man in the Dark (1940)

Babbacombe's (1941)

Under the Rainbow (1942)

Summer Pudding (1943)

Murder While You Work (1944)

Poppies for England (1948)

Pirouette (1948)

Love in a Mist (1951)

SUSAN SCARLETT

MURDER WHILE YOU WORK

With an introduction
by Elizabeth Crawford

DEAN STREET PRESS

A Furrowed Middlebrow Book

FM93

Published by Dean Street Press 2022

First published in 1944 by Hodder & Stoughton

Cover by DSP

ISBN 978 1 915393 24 1

www.deanstreetpress.co.uk

Introduction

WHEN reviewing *Clothes-Pegs*, Susan Scarlett's first novel, the *Nottingham Journal* (4 April 1939) praised the 'clean, clear atmosphere carefully produced by a writer who shows a rich experience in her writing and a charm which should make this first effort in the realm of the novel the forerunner of other attractive works'. Other reviewers, however, appeared alert to the fact that *Clothes-Pegs* was not the work of a tyro novelist but one whom *The Hastings & St Leonards Observer* (4 February 1939) described as 'already well-known', while explaining that this 'bright, clear, generous work', was 'her first novel of this type'. It is possible that the reviewer for this paper had some knowledge of the true identity of the author for, under her real name, Noel Streatfeild had, as the daughter of the one-time vicar of St Peter's Church in St Leonards, featured in its pages on a number of occasions.

By the time she was reincarnated as 'Susan Scarlett', Noel Streatfeild (1897-1986) had published six novels for adults and three for children, one of which had recently won the prestigious Carnegie Medal. Under her own name she continued publishing for another 40 years, while Susan Scarlett had a briefer existence, never acknowledged by her only begetter. Having found the story easy to write, Noel Streatfeild had thought little of *Ballet Shoes*, her acclaimed first novel for children, and, similarly, may have felt Susan Scarlett too facile a writer with whom to be identified. For Susan Scarlett's stories were, as the *Daily Telegraph* (24 February 1939) wrote of *Clothes-Pegs*, 'definitely unreal, delightfully impossible'. They were fairy tales, with realistic backgrounds, categorised as perfect 'reading for Black-out nights' for the 'lady of the house' (*Aberdeen Press and Journal*, 16 October 1939). As Susan Scarlett, Noel Streatfeild was able to offer daydreams to her readers, exploiting her varied experiences and interests to create, as her publisher advertised, 'light, bright, brilliant present-day romances'.

Noel Streatfeild was the second of the four surviving children of parents who had inherited upper-middle class values and expectations without, on a clergy salary, the financial means of realising them. Rebellious and extrovert, in her childhood and youth she had found many aspects of vicarage life unappealing, resenting both the restrictions thought necessary to ensure that a vicar's daughter behaved in a manner appropriate to the family's status, and the genteel impecuniousness and unworldliness that deprived her of, in particular, the finer clothes she craved. Her lack of scholarly application had unfitted her for any suitable occupation, but, after the end of the First World War, during which she spent time as a volunteer nurse and as a munition worker, she did persuade her parents to let her realise her dream of becoming an actress. Her stage career, which lasted ten years, was not totally unsuccessful but, as she was to describe on *Desert Island Discs*, it was while passing the Great Barrier Reef on her return from an Australian theatrical tour that she decided she had little future as an actress and would, instead, become a writer. A necessary sense of discipline having been instilled in her by life both in the vicarage and on the stage, she set to work and in 1931 produced *The Whicharts*, a creditable first novel.

By 1937 Noel was turning her thoughts towards Hollywood, with the hope of gaining work as a scriptwriter, and sometime that year, before setting sail for what proved to be a short, unfruitful trip, she entered, as 'Susan Scarlett', into a contract with the publishing firm of Hodder and Stoughton. The advance of £50 she received, against a novel entitled *Peter and Paul*, may even have helped finance her visit. However, the Hodder costing ledger makes clear that this novel was not delivered when expected, so that in January 1939 it was with *Clothes-Pegs* that Susan Scarlett made her debut. For both this and *Peter and Paul* (January 1940) Noel drew on her experience of occasional employment as a model in a fashion house, work for which, as she later explained, tall, thin actresses were much in demand in the 1920s.

Both *Clothes-Pegs* and *Peter and Paul* have as their settings Mayfair modiste establishments (Hanover Square and Bruton Street respectively), while the second Susan Scarlett novel, *Sally-Ann* (October 1939) is set in a beauty salon in nearby Dover Street. Noel was clearly familiar with establishments such as this, having, under her stage name 'Noelle Sonning', been photographed to advertise in *The Sphere* (22 November 1924) the skills of M. Emile of Conduit Street who had 'strongly waved and fluffed her hair to give a "bobbed" effect'. *Sally-Ann* and *Clothes-Pegs* both feature a lovely, young, lower-class 'Cinderella', who, despite living with her family in, respectively, Chelsea (the rougher part) and suburban 'Coulsden' (by which may, or may not, be meant Coulsdon in the Croydon area, south of London), meets, through her Mayfair employment, an upper-class 'Prince Charming'. The theme is varied in *Peter and Paul* for, in this case, twins Pauline and Petronella are, in the words of the reviewer in the *Birmingham Gazette* (5 February 1940), 'launched into the world with jobs in a

London fashion shop after a childhood hedged, as it were, by the vicarage privet'. As we have seen, the trajectory from staid vicarage to glamorous Mayfair, with, for one twin, a further move onwards to Hollywood, was to have been the subject of Susan Scarlett's debut, but perhaps it was felt that her initial readership might more readily identify with a heroine who began the journey to a fairy-tale destiny from an address such as '110 Mercia Lane, Coulsden'.

As the privations of war began to take effect, Susan Scarlett ensured that her readers were supplied with ample and loving descriptions of the worldly goods that were becoming all but unobtainable. The novels revel in all forms of dress, from underwear, 'sheer triple ninon step-ins, cut on the cross, so that they fitted like a glove' (*Clothes-Pegs*), through daywear, 'The frock was blue. The colour of hare-bells. Made of some silk and wool material. It had perfect cut.' (*Peter and Paul*), to costumes, such as 'a brocaded evening coat; it was almost military in cut, with squared shoulders and a little tailored collar, very tailored at the waist, where it went in to flare out to the floor' (*Sally-Ann*), suitable to wear while dining at the Berkeley or the Ivy, establishments to which her heroines – and her readers – were introduced. Such details and the satisfying plots, in which innocent loveliness triumphs against the machina-tions of Society beauties, did indeed prove popular. Initial print runs of 2000 or 2500 soon sold out and reprints and cheaper editions were ordered. For instance, by the time it went out of print at the end of 1943, *Clothes-Pegs* had sold a total of 13,500 copies, providing welcome royalties for Noel and a definite profit for Hodder.

Susan Scarlett novels appeared in quick succession, particularly in the early years of the war, promoted to readers as a brand; 'You enjoyed *Clothes-Pegs*. You will love Susan Scarlett's *Sally-Ann*', ran an advertisement in the *Observer* (5 November 1939). Both *Sally-Ann* and a fourth novel, *Ten Way Street* (1940), published barely five months after *Peter and Paul*, reached a hitherto untapped audience, each being serialised daily in the *Dundee Courier*. It is thought that others of the twelve Susan Scarlett novels appeared as serials in women's magazines, but it has proved possible to identify only one, her eleventh, *Pirouette*, which appeared, lusciously illustrated, in *Woman* in January and February 1948, some months before its book publication. In this novel, trailed as 'An enthralling story – set against the glittering fairyland background of the ballet', Susan Scarlett benefited from Noel Streatfeild's knowledge of the world of dance, while giving her post-war readers a young heroine who chose a husband over a promising career. For, common to most of the Susan Scarlett novels is the fact that the central figure is, before falling into the arms of her 'Prince Charming', a worker, whether, as we have seen, a Mayfair mannequin or beauty specialist, or a children's nanny, 'trained' in *Ten Way Street*, or, as in *Under the Rainbow* (1942), the untrained minder of vicarage orphans; in *The Man in the Dark* (1941) a paid companion to a blinded motor car racer; in *Babbacombe's* (1941) a department store assistant; in *Murder While You Work* (1944) a munition worker; in *Poppies for England* (1948) a member of a concert party; or, in *Pirouette*, a ballet dancer. There are only two exceptions, the first being the heroine of *Summer Pudding* (1943) who, bombed out of the London office in which she worked, has been forced to retreat to an archetypal southern English village. The other is *Love in a Mist* (1951), the final Susan

Scarlett novel, in which, with the zeitgeist returning women to hearth and home, the central character is a housewife and mother, albeit one, an American, who, prompted by a too-earnest interest in child psychology, popular in the post-war years, attempts to cure what she perceives as her four-year-old son's neuroses with the rather radical treatment of film stardom.

Between 1938 and 1951, while writing as Susan Scarlett, Noel Streatfeild also published a dozen or so novels under her own name, some for children, some for adults. This was despite having no permanent home after 1941 when her flat was bombed, and while undertaking arduous volunteer work, both as an air raid warden close to home in Mayfair, and as a provider of tea and sympathy in an impoverished area of south-east London. Susan Scarlett certainly helped with Noel's expenses over this period, garnering, for instance, an advance of £300 for *Love in a Mist*. Although there were to be no new Susan Scarlett novels, in the 1950s Hodder reissued cheap editions of *Babbacombe's*, *Pirouette*, and *Under the Rainbow*, the 60,000 copies of the latter only finally exhausted in 1959.

During the 'Susan Scarlett' years, some of the darkest of the 20th century, the adjectives applied most commonly to her novels were 'light' and 'bright'. While immersed in a Susan Scarlett novel her readers, whether book buyers or library borrowers, were able momentarily to forget their everyday cares and suspend disbelief, for as the reviewer in the *Daily Telegraph* (8 February 1941) declared, 'Miss Scarlett has a way with her; she makes us accept the most unlikely things'.

Elizabeth Crawford

CHAPTER I

JUDY sat staring out of the railway carriage window. Of course there was a war on, but could any train that was trying at all really dawdle the way this one was doing? Could there really be stations as small as the ones they were stopping at? The country was looking lovely, field after field of oats, rye and barley almost ready to cut. There was meadow-sweet waist high in the ditches, and dog-rose and honeysuckle springing out of the hedges. But Judy was tired; no one loved the country more than she did, but now she could think of nothing but the end of her journey. It was an end, too, from the look of things. When the journey had started the carriage had been jammed full of passengers, but one by one they had got out and left only herself and the studious young man. Judy took out her powder-case and had a look at her face and hair. Her nose was a little shiny, she decided, and her lips could stand a bit more lipstick, but her hair was all right. It was the sort that stayed where it was put; it was parted in the middle and with a slight wave on the top rippled nicely to her shoulders, where it fell in well-ordered curls. There were lots of things about herself that Judy would have changed, but not her hair. She was lucky over her hair and she knew it. Natural curls and waves as well as being red gold was a pretty decent helping for any girl's plate.

The train stopped at yet another little halt, and this time, perhaps because the driver was tired, it stopped so suddenly that Judy was almost thrown on the floor and her lipstick was actually thrown out of her hand. It went under the seat.

Judy, in a flash of thought, weighed the situation. The lipstick being round would have rolled as far under the seat as was possible. Its top was not on it so that an assortment of dust, half sandwiches, match-ends and bits of paper that live under railway carriages would by now have stuck to it. To retrieve it would mean hunting on the dirty carriage floor and, almost for a certainty, starting a ladder in her stockings. It was sickening to lose a lipstick which, because it was a present from an American, had been better than most, but it would be far worse to ladder a stocking. Maddening though it was, the lipstick would have to stay where it had rolled.

"Which side did it go?"

The studious young man who had seemed to Judy to take an interest in nothing but his heavy-looking book was half-way to the floor. Judy noticed how thin he was and how long-built to go grubbing under a railway seat.

"Don't bother. The top was off, things will have stuck to it."

He was kneeling on the floor. He raised his head. He was nice-looking in a sensitive, highly strung way, he had eyes as blue as Judy's own and a charming shy smile.

"But aren't they a bit hard to get? And it would clean, wouldn't it?"

Judy did not want to appear a helpless female. She was quite willing to believe it was a good role at the right time, but the right time was hardly the fourth year of a world war.

"It will, but I weighed it against my stockings. There's almost certainly grit on the floor and I simply can't face laddering them."

The young man accepted the stocking situation as a major issue, his face showed that he saw that a ladder could not be risked.

"Which side?" Judy told him. There was a pause while he searched. Then, in triumph, he passed the lipstick to her. "It is pretty dirty. Still, it's greasy, it would rub off on my paper."

Judy, having got back her lipstick, felt a sudden extra affection for it. She had seen men handle them before and knew that they thought it did no harm to break the paint away from the holder.

"I'll do it. As a matter of fact I think I'll have to do you too. Look at your knees! And there's a fluff of cotton wool or something on the back of your collar."

Obviously, after an introduction like that, the young man could not disappear back into his book. He closed it to show he had no intention of doing so. He gave Judy one of his shy, engaging smiles.

"Which is your station?"

"Pinlock."

He looked at her with interest.

"Are you coming to work there?"

Judy remembered all she had read and heard about careless talk. She answered him carefully.

"Yes. Not there exactly, but in the neighbourhood."

"It looks as if we were going to work under the same roof as it were."

Judy's eyes widened.

"Are we? Have you been directed here too?"

He laughed.

"The cat's out of the bag. There's no one to hear so we may as well speak the truth. You are going to work in Bigfields. I already work there."

Judy got up and sat down opposite him.

"No! What's it like? If it's simply foul you can tell me. I can take it. I've worked as a V.A.D. under what, before the war, was the matron of a workhouse and you can take anything after that."

He was a man who thought before he spoke.

"I don't know much about the women, but they look happy and all that. Of course the work is rather monotonous, but I suppose that's the same in all factories."

"And there's something about making munitions that gives you a kick, isn't there? I mean, everything else, nursing and all that, is useful, but you don't have the feeling that you are actually making the stuff that'll finish the war."

He took out his case and offered Judy a cigarette. He took one himself.

"I should have thought you couldn't be doing anything more useful than nursing."

She nodded, looking rather shame-faced.

"Too true. But, you see, I started while I was still at school, helping in the holidays and all that. Then, when I left school, I worked there altogether, and when I registered, the exchange said I could go on doing that unless they sent for me. Well, the hospital was for evacuated children, and by degrees there weren't many of them left, so they closed our hospital and sent our children to another one."

"So you were ordered to make shells."

Judy scowled at her cigarette.

"No, I wasn't. As a matter of fact they wanted me to go into another hospital and be properly trained, but I wouldn't. It sounds pretty shabby when nurses are needed, but I'm not a Florence Nightingale girl. I have tried to be, but the truth is I just hate nursing."

His eyes twinkled.

"So you're going to make shells! Have you got a billet?"

Judy opened her bag and produced a piece of paper.

"Mrs. Former," she read. "Old House, Longbottom Lane, Pinlock."

"Mrs. Former," he murmured thoughtfully. "Mrs. Former. I know the house, it's not far from the works."

"You said the bit about it not being far from the works in a different voice. What's wrong with Mrs. Former?"

"Nothing. It's just I can't place her. Somewhere at the back of my mind I know somebody has talked to me about her."

"And not said anything very nice."

He laughed.

"Your hearing is too acute. I can't remember what I heard about her. I just know somebody spoke about her to me."

Judy turned the piece of paper over.

"There's somebody else in the house. Clara Roal. Does that bring anything back to you?"

His face lit up.

"I hate not remembering names."

"Well, who said what?"

"It was nothing. There's a forewoman, a Mrs. White. She was billeted there. She happened to tell me that the old man in the house had died and she was going into a new billet."

Judy flicked the ash off her cigarette on to the floor.

"She said a lot more than that."

He sighed.

"If you must have it she said that she was glad to get out. That the house gave her the creeps. She's a townswoman and the place is lonely."

"We still haven't got to Clara Roal."

"What a girl you are for sticking to your point. Well, if you must know, Mrs. White disliked Mrs. Roal, but don't let it affect you. Mrs. White is a woman who likes everything in a house or a factory run her way, and I shouldn't think there's anybody she's been billeted on she hasn't had a few words with."

Having got her answer, Judy relaxed.

"I shan't care what Mrs. White thought. I never go by other people's opinions, and I certainly shan't mind the house being lonely. I've always lived in the country. As we've got so far do you mind me asking your name? Mine's Judy Rest."

"Nicholas Alexander Gordon Parsons."

"Gosh! You must have been the only son and they thought they'd christen you all the family favourites."

"No. I had two brothers. They both had several names. Dennis had five."

Judy's face was shocked.

"Had?"

"Dennis got his at Dunkirk and Lionel was brought down over Germany."

"Then . . ."

He stopped her.

"No. It was a crash, nobody had a chance to bail out."

"How awful! Your poor mother!"

"She's alone now. My father died some years ago. But she's busy, you know. Absolute prop and stay of the local W.V.S."

"What a mercy she's got you."

His face was half turned from Judy, but she could see his jaw muscles contract.

"Yes. I was the child who was too delicate to live. And now look at the damn thing. The sole survivor." She looked at his too fine skin and his long nervous hands, and the way his clothes hung on him.

"Are you all right now?"

"Ticking over nicely." He was opening his note-case. He took out a card and scribbled on it. "I work a bit away from the main factory, I'm doing some experimental stuff, but I'm getatable at the works on that number, and on this at the pub where I'm living. Park the card away somewhere and if you want anything, you know, don't like your job, or a bit fed up and lonely, or anything like wanting another billet, give me a ring." The train jerked to a stop. "This metropolis is Pinlock."

A local car had been hired to take Judy to her billet. Feeling rather lonely, she took out and turned over Nicholas' card. "The Honourable Nicholas Parsons," she read. She put the card carefully in her note-case. Her face was calm as she put it away, but her brain was turning over the order of Nicholas' words. If you want anything, and then he spoke of her job, being fed up or lonely, and last, as if it were an afterthought, her billet. She put the case away in her bag. "What is the matter with my billet? I'd swear he's heard something. Oh, well, Judy my girl, you'll soon find out!"

CHAPTER II

THE gloaming may be a good time for lovers, but is not, Judy decided, a good time for seeing your new billet after a long, tiring day. Old House lay at the end of a private road. "At least that's what old Mr. Former used to call it," the driver said to Judy. "I wouldn't call it a road myself, though if this was Blackpool they'd charge a shilling for a ride on it."

Old House, seen in the half light, seemed to be crouching back to hide amongst the trees that almost surrounded it. It was certainly old, originally Elizabethan, Judy decided, but repaired or brought up to date somewhere about the region of George the First.

"You may have to ring and knock," the driver said, "and go on ringing and knocking till someone answers. Mrs. Roal is out, I saw her up the village with the boy, and Mrs. Former is a bit deaf, and Miss Rose is a rare one for singing at her work and never hears anything no matter how hard you ring."

Judy found the driver's house knowledge to be quite accurate. First she rang and then she knocked, but nothing happened. From somewhere at the back came the squawking of chickens, there was a tremendous to-do among some rooks returning to their home in an elm on the lawn, but of human life not a sound.

"Try the back," the driver suggested. "Miss Rose is likely enough in the kitchen."

The back of the house was reached by a cobbled path and a small gate. The back door was open, there seemed no one in the kitchen, but singing came from an outhouse.

"A few more struggles here,
A few more partings o'er,
A few more toils,
A few more tears,
And we shall weep no more!"

Judy went to the door of the outhouse. A round-faced woman, with shiny cheeks and thin grey hair, was stooping over a bowl, pounding at something while she sang. She pounded so vigorously that the hymn came in doleful jerks. Judy stepped forward.

"Excuse me."

The woman started, the wooden spoon in her hand clattered into the bowl and she turned and faced Judy, her face crimson, one hand on her heart.

"Oh, sakes alive! You did give me a start, I thought you were Clara, you caught me red-handed. You're the lodger, I suppose."

"That's right, I'm Judy Rest. I did come to the front door of your house, but I couldn't make anyone hear."

The woman's eyes were roaming over Judy as if summing her up.

"Nobody would hear. Mother's out in the wood walking with Mr. Jones, and Clara has gone to Mr. Mutch to see if there's any honey from his bees this year. Last year was a terribly disappointing year for bees, and I do think the world of a drop of honey, don't you? It's because they were out that you caught me. I'd meant to be through before you arrived, but it's been slow to-day. Time slips by so, doesn't it?"

Judy approached the bowl and peered in and saw in the bottom some golden, very pre-war butter. "Goodness, that looks nice, Mrs. Former."

"Oh, my dear, you mustn't muddle me with Mother. Mother would never break the law. I'm Rose Former." She dropped her voice to a whisper. "Since you've caught me I may as well tell you the truth. Whenever there's a drop of milk over I pretend there isn't and then I put it on one side to set, and sometimes I make a little bit of butter, and sometimes I fancy a little drop of cream. Then Mother and I wait until Clara's out and we eat it. Of course we always lock the door, because you never know, do you? It's good for Mother really because she has her diabetes; she's allowed extra, but she can always do with a bit more. She's old, you know, and doesn't understand the rationing, if she did she'd die rather than let a bit pass her lips that wasn't rightly come by. I'm different. Somehow it seems I get an urge and I can't resist it. Clara keeps us very short, which is only natural with a child to feed, isn't it? Mind you, this milk isn't the child's, of course. When the farm can spare a bit extra I pay for it on the sly and pretend we've never had it."

The driver came to the door.

"Where am I going to put the bags, Miss Rose?"

Judy patted Miss Rose on the arm to show that she had grasped the need for secrecy.

"Let's stand them in the kitchen until Miss Rose is ready." She joined the driver outside. "How much do I owe you?"

He put the bags inside the back door and asked for three shillings. While Judy was getting out the money he leant towards her and lowered his voice to a whisper.

"The old lady's queer, Miss Rose is funny, and Mrs. Roal's the strangest of the lot. You haven't half come to a funny billet!"

Judy beamed at him as if he had handed her some good news. She gave him his money and a tip.

"Thank you so much. I do think a cheerful start makes such a difference, don't you? Good night."

Miss Rose came hurrying into the kitchen.

"I must just wash out this basin, dear, and then I'll take you up to your room. I lock the butter in the little cupboard in my bedroom." She glanced over her shoulder at Judy, who was standing by the window, the last of the light on her hair. "Dear me, you're very pretty, and so young. I do hope you'll be happy with us, but we're a dull house. Of course Clara's not very old, and there's Desmond. Desmond's eight, but he's a strange child, you know, so silent, it's not at all like having a child in the house."

Judy believed that only the neurotic allowed themselves to get fanciful about things, but she was beginning to admit to herself that her start in this house was hardly encouraging. She rather liked Miss Rose, even if, as the driver had said, she was a bit funny, but that Mrs. Roal who was not yet in should be the strangest of the lot, and Mrs. Former should be queer seemed a bit depressing, and now to hear of a child who was so strange that it was not like having a child in the house, hardly improved the outlook. "Never mind," she thought, "there is at least one person about whom I've heard nothing except that he's walking out with the old lady, and that's Mr. Jones. Let's hope that Mr. Jones is just another boarder like me and proves, even if dull, perfectly normal."

Miss Rose led the way up the creaking, rather rickety, wooden staircase to Judy's bedroom.

"Here, dear, this is where we put people billeted on us. I do hope you'll be happy and comfortable. Now, I'm just going to pop away and lock up the butter. Clara walks so quietly, you know."

Judy shut the door on Miss Rose and stared round her room. It was fairly large, long and low. In the centre of one wall was an enormous four-poster bed. Facing it on the other side was an equally large mahogany wardrobe. The window, which was at the narrow end of the room, faced the private road and the gate. "It's probably," thought Judy, "the only really ugly view in the house." Under the window there was a small rickety table with a little mirror standing on it, and by this an equally rickety chair. "I bet that's been added," Judy thought, "to make the room suitable for a female billetee." In the corner on the same side as the window there was a vast mahogany chest of drawers. There was just one really delightful piece of furniture. This was in the corner by the door, a little delicate washstand of mahogany with a fitted cream-coloured basin with pink roses running round it, and a cream-coloured waterewer standing in the basin with roses round its rim and on its handle. There were three pictures, all engravings. The Sermon on the Mount, the marriage at Cana and the miracle of the giant catch of fish. Judy looked up at the roof from which hung one naked electric-light bulb. "Well," she thought, "it couldn't possibly be in a worse place, it doesn't help the dressing-table, and you can't read in bed by it, but I should think it's pretty remarkable that there's electric light here at all. I could have taken a bet on a small piece of flickering candle." She knelt down beside her suitcases and unlocked them. "What you'd better do, my girl, is unpack. Nobody's ever said so far that Judy Rest ran away from anything, but if you look at this room too long you'll be letting your reputation down, and that's a certainty."

Her clothes hung in the wardrobe and packed away in the drawers, her hair combed, her face powdered, and her lips made up, and after the best wash she could manage in the cold water from the ewer, Judy, with her head up, came down the stairs prepared to face the household.

Miss Rose was in the kitchen working and singing.

"Oh, Paradise! Oh, Paradise!
The world is growing old:
Who would not be at rest and free . . ."

The singing stopped as Miss Rose saw Judy.

"There you are, dear. You'll find Mother in the drawing-room with Mr. Jones, first door on the left."

She lowered her voice to a whisper. "Not a word about the butter mind."

By the drawing-room window in an armchair sat a frail old lady knitting, and at her feet, snoring abominably, was a small black pug dog. There was nobody else in the room and Judy looked resignedly at the dog. "I might have known it," she thought; "this is just the kind of house to raise a girl's hopes by railing their dog Mr. Jones." She came forward to the old lady and lifted her voice.

"How do you do, Mrs. Former? I'm Judy Rest. You know, I'm billeted on you."

Mrs. Former was slow in her movements and apparently slow in her thinking. She laid down her knitting, and after a pause smiled at Judy.

"Of course, I remember, you're going to be billeted here, you're going to work at the factory making munitions."

Judy looked round the room at the relics of bygone years. The bead stools, the ornaments, the embroidered fire-screen, the wax flowers under a glass cover, the dents in the chairs made by long sitting in one position, and she felt pity for the old lady. It could not be much fun to go on living in a room that you had shared for years with somebody who was now dead. Old Mr. Former had probably brought Mrs. Former to this room as a bride. In the winter nights they sat facing each other in those twin armchairs by the fireplace, discussing what they would do with their children, or was Miss Rose the only child? Anyway, it must be pretty dreary now, a little deaf, a little out of things, sitting by yourself, the last of your generation, and it could not add to things to have a strange girl billeted on you.

"I shan't be much trouble. I have to be at the factory by eight and I don't leave the works until six, so I shan't be in very much except just Saturday afternoons and Sundays."

Mrs. Former stared up at Judy, obviously turning over what she had said.

"But, my dear child, I'm delighted to have you. We were always willing to have somebody; we always have had somebody, it's only since Mr. Former died that we have had nobody. It was a shock, you know. We had never thought him ill, he was only a little run down. Doctor Mead was so kind, my husband was so tiresome about medicine that he arranged to have his injected. You see, he was accustomed to injections. I take insulin." The old lady's voice rose in pride. "I've learnt to give it to myself. I don't believe in being dependent. Clara, of course, looked after my husband. Clara's a splendid nurse."

Judy thought this was a good occasion to sort out Clara. "Is Clara your granddaughter?"

"By marriage, my only one. We had two daughters, Rose and Millicent. Millicent married a very nice man called Roal, but Mr. Former never quite approved of the marriage because her husband was a chemist. Such a lovely shop, those great big bottles in the window all scarlet and green, but Mr. Former was a vet, you know, and vets are, of course, in a socially different world to chemists."

Judy still wanted a line on Clara.

"Then Clara is your daughter Millicent's daughter?" The old lady looked slightly hurt.

"No, indeed. Clara is not at all like my family. So business-like, you know. No, she married Alfred, Millicent's son. Millicent had only the one boy. She died soon after he was born. When his father died Alfred inherited the shop, such a nice business, so sad to think of it being smashed by one of those nasty bombs. Clara was there first thing in the morning and she said it was a dreadful sight, glass everywhere."

"Nobody hurt, I hope," said Judy.

The old lady shook her head.

"No, nobody except Alfred, he was killed, just blown to pieces, Clara says. I'm so glad that when Mr. Former had to go it was not that way, so unseemly, I think. I do like a grave, don't you, dear?"

Judy had no very strong views on burials so she changed the subject. "So lucky for Mrs. Roal that she had your home to come to."

"I don't think she thinks herself lucky. She has always disliked it here very much indeed."

Like so many deaf people Mrs. Former spoke more loudly than was necessary. Judy was glad the door was shut. It would be a tiresome beginning with Mrs. Roal if she found the lodger gossiping about her with her grandmother-in-law.

She knelt down by Mr. Jones and patted him.

"What a nice dog!"

"He gets asthma; I'm deaf so I don't hear him wheezing. Clara says he makes a terrible noise." The old lady's eyes grew anxious. "I feel nervous sometimes that she thinks he should be destroyed, but he's such a companion and does so enjoy his food."

Mr. Jones was wheezing, but contentedly. Judy would have liked to have taken Mrs. Former's hand and squeezed it, instead she gave her a friendly smile.

"I think he looks splendid. Nobody could want to destroy him."

Mrs. Former looked slightly cheered, but her eyes were still anxious.

"Clara might. She's so practical and capable. More like a man really. I have always been foolish, I've never understood business. Mr. Former never spoke to me about it, he knew I wouldn't understand. Sometimes he spoke about his sick animals, but not about money, but he left me provided for. He always said that if he should be taken before I was I would find everything was all right, and it has been. Mr. John, our lawyer, said his arrangements were splendid. Mr. Former found it difficult to understand Clara. He could not understand a woman who was interested in business, but Clara is so clever, she kept trying to persuade my husband to do things with his money which she said would make him richer, but he never would; in fact, he got angry."

"I don't wonder," thought Judy, "it was a bit of sauce from a grandchild-in-law." Out loud she said, still hoping to get off the subject of Clara,

"It must be an interesting life being a vet. Making sick animals well."

"Oh, very, and he was splendid, everybody said so. In peace-time he used to be sent for from all over the country, he was particularly clever about bulls. I never quite understood in what way and it's not a subject for a young girl. Very large fees he earned. I so remember the day when he bought the house and land. 'It's yours for ever, Mollykins,' he said, that's what he called me, 'and after that it will belong to Rose, and after that to Millicent's grandson.' He rather hoped Desmond might become a vet, but he's a funny child. Mr. Former used to forget how young he is and lose patience with him."

"It's nice you have this lovely house."

Mrs. Former looked round wistfully.

"Yes, but it's not the same since Mr. Former was taken. I had always hoped to go first. But I'm very fortunate I have dear Rose and, of course, Clara is a wonderful manager. She arranges everything."

A creak behind her made Judy look round. The door was opening and in it stood a thin dark girl. Judy scrambled up from the floor.

"How do you do? I was just making friends with Mr. Jones. I'm Judy Rest and you must be Mrs. Roal." Clara shook Judy's hand.

"Yes." She was silent a second while she looked Judy over. "Have you seen your room?"

"She's rather pretty, or perhaps handsome is a better word," thought Judy. "If her eyes weren't too close together she'd be downright lovely."

"Yes, thank you, and I've unpacked. I've been telling your grandmother I shan't be troubling you much. I have to be at the factory at eight and I don't stop work until six."

"Yes, we know. We've had people billeted before." Clara smiled kindly. "I expect you're tired, supper will soon be ready."

Judy felt that Clara was misunderstood, she obviously meant to be friendly.

"That's good. It's a long journey here, or rather, the train's so slow."

"Pinlock hadn't a station before the war, it's only been put up for the works. It's a very isolated place, at least to me, but then I'm used to London; but perhaps you're used to it, you've come from another factory, haven't you?"

"No. This is my first effort in that line. I've been working in a hospital."

Clara had been straightening a chair cover while she talked. On Judy's last words her hand stopped moving as if it were suddenly paralysed.

"A hospital!" She hesitated, then crossed to the old lady. "Come on, Grandmother, supper will be ready." She smiled over her shoulder at Judy. "We live in a very old-fashioned way. Granny and Aunt Rose are used to it, but it will be dull for you. I'll have a rake round and see if I can get you billeted somewhere brighter."

CHAPTER III

Judy woke with a start and the strange feeling of not knowing where she was, then through her sleep-drugged brain she heard knocking on her door. On her call of "Come in" Clara, fully dressed, came to the bedside with a cup of tea.

"It's half-past six."

Judy pushed her hair off her face. She sat up and stared at Clara.

"Whatever time do you get up?"

Clara was pulling back the curtains.

"Half-past five. There's a lot to do, you know, in a house this size, and Desmond wakes early."

Judy sipped her tea.

"Oh, yes, Desmond, I haven't met him yet."

"I don't think it's good for children to mix too much with adults, so I usually give him his meals by himself, he's very highly strung. Unusually brilliant. I don't send him to school, he's taught privately."

Although it was early morning and Judy was half asleep, she was not so half asleep but she tried to sort out these statements. There was a vast difference between one story and another. Miss Rose had said that Desmond was such a silent child, having him was not like having a child in the house at all. Mrs. Former had said that Mr. Former used to forget how young Desmond was and lose patience with him. None of it fitted somehow with Clara's "unusually brilliant". It probably was because the child was highly strung, old people would not be likely to understand that sort of temperament, they would not want to be bothered with moods.

"I'm glad there's a child in the house," she said cheerfully. "I like children. If he's highly strung he's probably interesting."

Clara came to the bed foot. She leant against one of the posts.

"This isn't the house for you. You're young and pretty, and ought to have a good time."

Judy grinned at her.

"Well, you're not so old yourself, and I can't see anything the matter with your face."

Clara was looking down at her hands. She twiddled her wedding-ring round her finger.

"I don't want anything. My life's finished, I only live for Desmond."

She said this last sentence with such intensity that Judy's eyes were full of pity. How fond she must have been of her Alfred, who was blown to pieces in his chemist's shop! How appalling for poor Clara to have been so early on the scene! Mrs. Former's "it was a dreadful sight" probably covered a lot. She tried to think of something comforting to say.

"Such a mercy you've Desmond. I think it must help a little when there's a child."

Clara gave her a quick look, as if to see if she were being sincere or not, which Judy found queer. It was hardly likely that somebody would be insincere in sympathizing over an awful thing like that. Clara, as if impatient with herself, made a quick dive at Judy's empty cup. Her voice was abrupt.

"Well, I mustn't stand here gossiping or you'll never be up in time. The bath water's hottish, if you can't bear it come to the landing and shout over and I'll bring you up a kettle."

Judy met Desmond in the lane on her way to work. She saw ahead of her a thin dark little boy wearing a canary yellow shirt and shorts. She ran after him to catch him up.

"Hullo! Are you Desmond?"

The child gave her a blank stare.

"Say?"

Judy repeated her question, and added:

"I'm sure you are because you're very like your mother."

Desmond stared at Judy with an enraptured expression, but was not apparently taking in what she said.

"There's a place down the spinney where I saw a boggart."

Judy searched her brain to remember what a boggart was.

"An elf?"

"He's all brown like earth and his eyes is blue like bits of sky."

"Where d'you go to your lessons?"

"Mr. Mutch has a new car."

Judy looked down at Desmond. "If this child were mine," she thought, "he would have no meals at all until he answered when he was spoken to." However, she was not going to let somebody of eight beat her, so she struggled on.

"Look, this is my case to carry my things to the works, it's new to-day."

"They've dug a new hole in the churchyard. Last time they put great-grandad in."

"Well, the new one won't be for him, they won't want to put him in again." She gripped Desmond by the arm. "I was showing you my case, what do you think of it?"

Desmond raised his head.

"That there's a lark singing, sometimes he sings so loud he busts. I saw a note that a lark had sung come down once after a lark had burst."

Judy remembered thankfully that Clara had said that Desmond did not mix much with adults. Clara had said it was because grown-up people were not good for Desmond, but it seemed to her to stand out a mile that Desmond was not good for grown-up people. She found herself in the ridiculous position of being annoyed with him. However, she let go his arm and struggled with the question of the burst lark.

"What does a lark's note look like when it comes down after the lark's burst?"

"I don't go to an ordinary school because of letters. I don't read them. Mum says she understands why I don't, but the school wouldn't."

Judy looked at the child with a fresh eye.

"Surely you know some of your letters, don't you? You're eight. You must at least know the alphabet."

They had come to cross-roads. One led downhill with a winding grass-bordered path, the other was a high road, up which rows of men and girls were streaming on foot and on bicycles. Desmond turned down the grass-bordered track.

"A butterfly can sing if you sit very quiet to hear it." Judy thankfully left him and joined the stream of men and girls.

"If I'd been that taxi-driver last night," she thought, "it's not Mrs. Former and Miss Rose and Clara that I'd have said queer and funny. Of course Clara may be right and that child shows unusual brilliance, but to me he's just plain strange."

The hours of that first day at the factory seemed interminable. The whirring of thousands of straps, the turning of thousands of lathes, the banging, the hammering. Dimly Judy heard the instructions screamed into her ear as to how to work her lathe. At twelve o'clock a hooter, so loud that it beat all the other noises in the factory, howled, and Judy followed the example of the rest of the workers, who had taken up their place in a queue leading to the canteen. The works' canteen was vast. On a tray you collected your lunch and took it to a table; it was a good lunch, hot joint and two vegetables, and a pudding and a cup of tea, all for one and four-pence, but Judy was almost too tired to eat it. At twelve-thirty the canteen wireless was turned on. At her hospital the wireless was not used a great deal, and she had no idea how music could help. It was extraordinary, she found, what the swinging tunes did to straighten your back and take the ache out of your feet.

The patch from one o'clock to half-past three, when the tea-wagon came round, Judy found intolerable. Her head ached from the noise, her feet ached from standing, and her hands ached from gripping the capstan handle. Her fellow workers were as kind as they could be, but each one had to work hard and each one was tired. During the afternoon her lathe jammed and the setter was sent for. He repaired it for ten exquisite minutes while Judy sat in a heap on a box.

"Gets you at first," said the setter.

"It shouldn't get me," Judy retorted. "I've been working in a hospital and, believe me, there's nothing about the use of the feet that a nurse doesn't know."

"That's right," agreed the setter, "but it's the noise here, see? We got over a thousand lathes working, and over there," he jerked his thumb to the opposite side of the factory, "there's over a thousand women gauging, and though gauging don't make much noise their tongues do. I tell my mate I'd rather have another thousand lathes than them. Then, outside, there's the shell-filling, and beyond that the experimental huts." Judy's face lit up.

"Have you met a Mr. Parsons who experiments here?"

"Nick Parsons. I'd just about say I have. Do you know him?"

"No, we travelled on the train together yesterday, he seemed nice."

The setter nodded.

"I'll say he's nice, and he's brave too. He works by himself on something you and me mustn't know nothing about, but it's so damned explosive that just covering it in with grass like they usually do wasn't enough, and they built a great blast-proof wall round it. They say hereabouts that if what Nick Parsons is working on comes off, and is got into production, Hitler'll eat all the carpets left in Germany." He moved away from the lathe. "There you are, dear, you don't want to jerk too much, work the thing more smooth. Try humming as you turn the turret. The girls in this group say that 'White Christmas' just swings it nicely." He was moving off when a thought struck him. "Mr. Parsons asked me to make him a little tool he wants, and I got to speak to him about it on the phone presently. Shall I tell him I've seen you and that you've settled down all right?"

Judy gave the setter a lovely smile.

"Yes. My name's Judy Rest. Tell him that I'm getting along all right, and what I'm working on."

The setter moved off down the aisle whistling. The tune he was whistling was "I'll walk beside you", but his mind was saying, "If that Nick Parsons has hooked that bit of skirt, he's a different boy to what we took him for. That's one of the tastiest bits of crackling that's come inside this factory since we opened."

The last stretch, from the departure of the tea-wagon to knock-off, passed in a muzzy dream of fatigue for Judy. She hummed as the setter had suggested, but she was a long way past realizing she was doing it. Nevertheless, because of the humming of "White Christmas", or through sheer exhaustion, she was becoming mechanical, her work improved. Her arms and feet moved with rhythm, and the small pieces of shell case on which she was working dropped into their container with a speed and regularity which would have been impossible to her in the morning.

"Pretty good!"

Judy swung round. The words had been said in her ear and made her jump. Nicholas was standing behind her. He had on grey flannel trousers and a white shirt, and looked cool and clean. Judy, conscious of a sticky, probably dirty, certainly unpowdered face, glared at him.

"So splendid our girls, aren't they? England's proud of them."

His smile lit up his face.

"As a matter of fact you do look rather like a poster. You know, 'The girl behind the gun'."

"I bet I do, shining nose and all." She looked at her machine. "Well, I mustn't waste time. This horror needs constant attention."

He directed her eyes to the girls around her. "It's knock-off and clean-up."

Judy turned. A few of the girls were still working, but the majority had a lump of waste in their hands and were cleaning their machines. One of the girls saw Judy's enquiring look and came over. Nicholas grinned at her.

"Hullo, Shirley, how's the voice?" He turned to Judy. "This is the factory soprano. I'm the accompanist. Shirley has had a lot to put up with."

Shirley giggled.

"Give over, Mr. Parsons!" She turned her attention to Judy. "You get waste and some oil from that hatch. You sweep all the filings into that box and, as they say, leave your machine as you'd wish to find it. Matter of fact, it's you who'll do the finding, there's no night work on this group at present."

Judy thanked Shirley. "She's nice," she told Nicholas. "She's helped me all day."

He turned to go.

"I live at The Bull, you can't miss it. It's opposite the church. Come and have a cocktail, it will give you the strength to get home."

"A cocktail! Could I do with one! But I mustn't be late."

"You won't. Get cracking at that cleaning and be ready to run as soon as you hear the hooter."

The Bull was a nice old place, evidently originally a coaching inn. Judy found Nicholas in the bar parlour. He had two cocktails on a table.

"It's gin and lime. I had to guess what you'd like. Not that there's much choice, and, of course, more days than not there's no gin. We're lucky to-night."

Judy sank thankfully into a chair.

"I suppose you get used to making yourself heard above the noise of the machines, but I feel now as if I must shout."

"You won't even need to shout in the works in time. It's pitch. You'll get it."

Judy looked around at the rest of the bar users. She thought she was being furtively stared at.

"Is it the custom for the likes of me to drink with the likes of you?"

"I've no idea and I certainly don't care. How's the billet?"

Judy took the cigarette he offered her.

"Well, I wouldn't call it home from home. I mean, I shan't go scampering up the road saying, 'Goody, goody, there's my dear billet waiting for me'."

"What are the family like?"

"There's old Mrs. Former. She's rather a pet, a bit talkative. She's got a wheezing, aged dog called Mr. Jones. I'm sorry for Mrs. Former, I think she misses her husband. He was a vet who specialized in treating bulls."

"That's the old fellow who died suddenly a few weeks ago."

"That's him. Then there's daughter Rose. She's rather a pet too. Does the cooking and sings hymns at the top of her voice."

"And what about Mrs. Roal?"

Judy fixed her eyes on his.

"I would love to know why you are curious about Mrs. Roal."

"I'm not."

"You are. I don't think you know it. Perhaps it's left you interested."

"Well, what is she like?"

"Young. Nice looking. Her mother-in-law was Millicent, Miss Rose's sister. She married a man called Roal, who was a chemist. They had a son called Alfred, who was this Clara's husband. Alfred was killed by a bomb which hit his shop. Clara's got a boy called Desmond. He's eight. She says he's brilliant. I should say he was simple, and that's being over-generous."

"What's the house like?"

"Old and could be lovely, actually it's like living in grandmother's photograph album. Nothing's missing. Mantelpieces with bits of stuff hanging off them, ghastly ornaments, all the lot." She got up. "I ought to be going. I don't want to get a bad reputation to start off with. They've had people billeted on them before, as you know, and they've grasped exactly what hours one ought to keep."

He finished his drink.

"I'll walk with you a bit of the way. The air will give me an appetite for my fried spam."

It was a lovely evening, the road was almost deserted for the workers had mostly gone home. Judy took a deep breath.

"It smells good, doesn't it? Is the country nice round here?"

"Lovely. About a mile in any direction and you are out in the open. This factory is a war-time growth. It was small to start with, but it was expanded after Bristol was bombed. But Pinlock, in spite of the grandeur of a railway halt, is just a sleepy, self-contained village, and it won't surprise me if, after the last enemy has been shown what happens to people who make war on their neighbours, it slips back into being just Pinlock again. I think even the station will disappear. The people hereabouts prefer the bus."

"What does one do for entertainment?"

"If you don't mind being crushed and standing all the way you can go to Bristol. Once in a while E.N.S.A. gives us a show, but mostly we amuse ourselves. Dances, whist drives, concerts, theatricals, you wouldn't believe what a whirl of gaiety we live in."

They had come to the cross-roads. As they left the high road and turned up the lane leading to the private road to Old House, a sigh escaped Judy. It was quite a loud sigh and she hurried to laugh it away.

"Sad to hear me, isn't it?"

Nicholas said nothing for a moment, then he gave her one of his nicest smiles.

"The thought of home getting you down?"

She squared her shoulders.

"Anything would and, anyway, home my foot. I'm tired. So would anybody be at the end of their first day in a factory."

They walked on in silence until they reached the private road. Then Nicholas stopped.

"I shan't come any farther. Perhaps one Saturday you could get me invited to tea. Have they said anything about followers?"

Judy suddenly felt horribly forlorn, but not for worlds would she let him see it.

"No, but I expect it can be arranged. Good night, Mr. Parsons."

He hesitated as if he wanted to say something. Then he changed his mind.

"Good night, Miss Rest."

CHAPTER IV

"'Twas on a Sunday morning
That I beheld my darling,
She looked so sweet and charming
In every high degree.
She looked so sweet and charming-o
A-wearing of her linen-o."

JUDY leant against a tree.

"Just fancy meeting you!" She touched her frock. "But it's not linen. This is *crêpe de Chine* I'd have you know. Practically the last pure silk in the world."

Nicholas propped himself against another tree.

"Whatever it is, that bright yellow and your red hair against those brown tree-trunks is a refreshment to the eye."

"Thank you. Don't you say your piece nicely! And your singing!"

"I'm considered to have a very nice voice. At our works' concert, at which, as you know, I'm an accompanist, my name is scarcely ever off the announcer's tongue. 'Mr. Nick Parsons, our whispering baritone.' Loud laughter, as they say in Parliament."

Judy moved a few steps from her tree.

"Talking of voices, can you hear a wheeze? Mr. Jones is out with me." She raised her voice. "Mr. Jones. Mr. Jones."

The pug came pushing through some bracken. He wheezed abominably, but was a picture of dog-like bliss. Nicholas snapped his fingers at him.

"Hullo, old man! Bit on the fat side, isn't he?"

Judy came back to her tree.

"For goodness' sake don't say so. Mr. Jones' food is a very delicate subject."

"Why?"

"Officially he has nothing that's suitable for human consumption. Actually he has meat and two veg on the sly almost every day of the week."

"How does he get it?"

"Oh, you know, the old lady does without a bit and Miss Rose sneaks snippets, and the butcher, who's an old friend, saves scraps. Even the billetee helps. If I've a bit over on my plate in the canteen I usually bring it home for him."

"Well, who's grudging the poor old boy his pickings?"

"Our Clara. But not only Mr. Jones, it's all of us. You wouldn't believe the things that go on in our house. The underground movement in France is nothing to what we're up to."

Nicholas sat down and pulled Mr. Jones to him.

"How?"

"Milk is our chief secret weapon. The milkman, another old friend, sometimes has a bit over, and when he does he's paid in cash for it so it shan't show on the books, and then we lock all the doors and put on a guard to watch out for Clara, and we skim ourselves a little cream, or, if there's enough milk, we've been known to make an ounce of butter. To-day for lunch Mrs. Former and Miss Rose and I are having a picnic. We've got two sandwiches each of very thinly spread potted meat, at least that's what Clara thinks, but she doesn't know how the minds of the subjugated work; we've got a cold chicken."

Nicholas ran a finger up Mr. Jones' spine.

"But whose house is it?"

"Mrs. Former's, but she doesn't have any say, poor old pet. Clara is the managing sort. And I must say she's too efficient for words, and as for hard work, my day is a life of ease compared to Clara's!"

"Whose money is it?"

"Mrs. Former's. Clara has a bit, but it's being saved for Desmond. But, mind you, when you say money, we hardly ever spend any. Clara sees to that. Poor old Mrs. Former isn't even allowed to use her clothing coupons." Nicholas' fingers moved delicately up Mr. Jones' back. The dog shuddered with pleasure.

"What's happening to Clara during the picnic?"

"Feeding Desmond." Judy scratched some fallen pine needles with her toe. "Did you ever hear that eating an awful lot was a sign of being a lunatic?"

Nicholas stared at her.

"Yes, but Clara doesn't sound like that."

"Not her. Desmond. That's what's at the back of all this meanness about food. It's hateful really, nobody ever gets their full ration of anything, or wouldn't if Miss Rose wasn't a wonderful pilferer." She hesitated, obviously considering whether she would say something.

Nicholas smiled up at her.

"Out with it."

"Well, one day I was passing the kitchen while Desmond was having his lunch. It was frightening. Shovel, shovel. I didn't know a child of eight could eat so much, and as his plate emptied Clara piled on some more."

"How peculiar is the kid?"

"Oddly enough, although I've been in the house over a week, I've only spoken to him once, that morning after I arrived. I must say I thought him very strange indeed."

Nicholas' fingers paused at their stroking.

"How ghastly for the wretched Clara."

Judy sat down by him.

"Awful. It makes me feel such a cad for not liking her."

"But you can't?"

Judy picked up a few pine needles and sprinkled them on Mr. Jones' back.

"No. I believe if I was the sort of person who could be frightened, she'd frighten me. I don't know why. But there's something about her."

Nicholas carefully picked the pine needles off Mr. Jones.

"If I ate nothing but potted meat sandwiches couldn't I come to the picnic?"

Judy was suddenly conscious of the sunlight through the trees, the smell of bracken, the gay little cries of birds, and the fluttering of the leaves on the tree-tops as a breeze went by. Nicholas had been right when he had said the country round about was lovely. She had been right to come to a factory. How she was liking it! How gay she felt! How gorgeous this Sunday morning was being! It must be the joy of a day outside and the quietness after a week of unending noise.

"I don't see why not. Mrs. Former and Miss Rose have gone to church. Miss Rose has the picnic-basket, it's being left in charge of the verger. It's from him that she's bought the chicken and his wife cooked it, we didn't dare have it up at the house. There's a meadow below the church. We're meeting there."

"Aren't you afraid of Clara taking a walk and spotting you?"

Judy got up laughing.

"Terribly. But subjugated people get so tough, you wouldn't believe. Come on, it's time we were moving."

They heard the picnic-party before they saw them. Miss Rose was singing:

"Jerusalem, my happy home,
Name ever dear to me,
When shall my labours have an end?
Thy joys when shall . . ."

She broke off and raised her voice. "There, Mother dear, isn't that a lovely bird and so beautifully cooked. I don't know when I last had a real good eat of chicken."

The meadow was soft underfoot. Judy and Nicholas made no noise as they walked along. Judy picked up Mr. Jones and drew Nicholas off the path.

"They're behind that tree. Let's creep up quietly. I want you to see them as they are and not with their party manners. They really are ducks."

With her back to the tree-trunk Mrs. Former was sitting on a camp-stool. She was wearing her better black summer dress and an old lady's hat of black straw with a mauve velvet bow. On her knee lay her hymn and prayer book and her gloves. Miss Rose was on her knees laying out a handful of dock leaves into a square.

"There, that looks nice, doesn't it? I wish I could have brought a table-cloth, but I didn't dare, it might have made Clara wonder. You hardly need a cloth for sandwiches. Let alone she thinks we're having them in the churchyard." She looked up at her mother. "I'm glad it's such a lovely day for little Judy. We don't want her getting pale in that factory."

Mrs. Former leaned towards Rose.

"Can you see the clock, dear? I think Judy's late. I hope she has found her way."

Judy could not bear that, she came forward from behind the tree. She laid a hand on Mrs. Former's shoulder.

"Here I am." She put Mr. Jones on the ground and crouched by Miss Rose. "I've brought a visitor, I hope you don't mind."

Nicholas came forward.

"But he only wants potted meat sandwiches."

Judy introduced him, he sat down by Mrs. Former's stool. "I've been making friends with Mr. Jones. I hope you are going to spare him a little bit of chicken."

Mrs. Former was clearly delighted.

"You are fond of dogs, Mr. Parsons? How very nice. My granddaughter-in-law thinks that perhaps we should not allow ourselves the pleasure of a dog in wartime, an extra mouth, you know, but Mr. Jones has never been at all a gross feeder, even when he could have everything of the best, which, of course, he did when my husband was alive because he was a vet, you know."

"I do hope," Miss Rose broke in, "that Judy has warned you, Mr. Parsons, that you'll have to eat with your fingers. We left home meaning to lunch on sandwiches, the chicken has been a great surprise."

Nicholas gave her one of his best smiles.

"I understand the situation perfectly, but the sandwiches will do for me, I came on that understanding."

"Nonsense!" Miss Rose eyed the chicken thoughtfully. "I have brought a sharp kitchen knife and this fork to carve it, but as you're here perhaps you would do it. Gentlemen are so much cleverer at these things. My father would never let Mother or me touch a joint, and as for a ham – he would hardly let us near it!"

Mrs. Former patted Nicholas on the shoulder.

"Yes, you carve. My husband was a beautiful carver."

Nicholas crawled round the dock-leaf table-cloth and took the knife and fork from Miss Rose.

"Do you know, this picnic is one of the nicest things that's happened to me since I came to Pinfold. We mustn't let Judy think it's often like this, must we?"

Judy looked across the meadow which was shimmering with heat. Below them was a stream singing along, a blue thread between reeds and meadow-sweet. Behind them amongst the trees was the square tower of the church. Overhead, singing its heart out, was a lark, and under the tree a queer, ill-assorted little party gently happy.

"It couldn't often be like this." Judy felt she had spoken with more warmth than the occasion seemed to excuse. She explained herself. "I mean, it's not often such a divine day."

Nicholas passed Mrs. Former some chicken on a dock leaf.

"Make very good plates these dock leaves do. My mother would approve of them. Amongst other things she's a pillar of the Women's Institute. Nobody living can have thought out more ways of using things for other purposes than that for which they were designed than my mother."

"Well, isn't that nice," said Miss Rose. "I do like to see people being clever with their fingers. Does she make pretty things with fir cones and that?"

Nicholas and Judy did not dare look at each other for fear they would smile and their smiles be misinterpreted. It was perfectly true that Miss Rose amused them, but they were not laughing at her, but loving her for the simple, unaffected creature that she was.

They finished the chicken down to the last fragment, Mr. Jones having his fair share, when Mrs. Former leant forward and looked pleadingly at Nicholas.

"I do hope you will forgive me, Mr. Parsons. I know gentlemen don't like being asked questions after a meal, but there is a little business point, at least I think it's business, on which I would be so glad of your advice. Is there any way in which a small sum of money could be regularly taken from my bank account and sent through the post without my visiting the bank or writing a cheque?"

Nicholas gave himself and Judy a cigarette before he answered.

"From that question you think somebody is taking money from you?"

Mrs. Former gazed at him with the face of a shocked child.

"Oh, dear, no! Who would dream of robbing me? Everybody's always so kind. No, it's an old friend. During my husband's lifetime I always sent her little sums to help her along and he quite agreed that I should. But Clara says now, that with death-duties, I can't afford a single extravagance, and I dare say that's true, but, you see, I must help my friend, she relies on it."

Nicholas moved closer to the old lady so that he did not need to shout.

"But what does your bank manager say? Is he worrying about the overdraft or anything?"

Mrs. Former shook her head.

"I never see him. I should never dare. My husband always said I was silly about business, and I'm sure he was perfectly right. He left everything in the hands of Mr. John, our lawyer, and I'm mercifully well provided for."

Miss Rose broke in.

"Clara, my niece by marriage, you know, is such a wonderful manager that we leave everything to her. Mother and I are rather stupid about money and it makes Clara cross. You can't blame her. I expect you'll think this very silly, Mr. Parsons, but Mother and I are a little afraid of Clara so we do things behind her back. It's naughty of us, I know, for she is so clever and so good to us, but when she's angry with Mother, it makes Mother all of a shake."

Mrs. Former flushed.

"I'm such a silly old woman, and very easily upset since my husband was taken. I haven't many years to live, Mr. Parsons, and I would like to live them peacefully. If you know of any way by which I might get this money to my friend I should be so grateful."

Nicholas frowned. He scratched a little hole in the field.

"You can quite easily send money to your friend by a banker's order. Once that's fixed up it's a sum regularly deducted from your account, and it will go on being deducted until you say stop. But if you don't mind my saying so, however clever your granddaughter may be, you don't want her to dominate you. Your husband left you provided for so that you should enjoy yourself."

Mrs. Former looked at Miss Rose as if for encouragement. Miss Rose struggled for words.

"We sound foolish, I know, but I'm afraid we must admit that Clara being so modern and so clever frightens us a little. We should not enjoy ourselves if Clara was angry with us."

A cloud passed across the sun and threw a shadow over the picnic-party. Judy gave a shiver. Nicholas turned to look at her as if sensing that something was wrong. She got up and straightened her frock.

"Time I moved, a goose has walked over my grave. Come on, Nick, let's take the chicken carcase to somebody's dustbin."

It's extraordinary, in the middle of a war where the entire nation has become dustbin-minded, how difficult it is to find a secluded dustbin. Nicholas almost gave up the search.

"I feel this must be rather like trying to bury a body. There can't be any harm in putting the chicken into a dustbin, can there?"

Judy had the carcase wrapped in dock leaves.

"Not to you, but if you were a subjugated race you would get cautious. The very last thing we want is someone saying brightly to Clara, 'Fancy now, that young lady that's billeted with you left a chicken carcase in my dustbin'." She caught at Nicholas' sleeve. "Look! What do I see outside that door up that turning?"

"And very nice too. As pretty a dustbin as ever I set eyes on, and a good thing too as we're nearly home." Trying to look casual they sauntered up the turning. Nicholas looked at the surrounding windows. There was not a face about. He took off the dustbin lid.

"And a very nicely kept dustbin. I think it's meant for pig food, but our chicken will probably be isolated by the thrifty owner and put in its proper place."

Judy pulled the dock leaves off the carcase.

"In you go and let's hope there are no finger-prints." She felt a pull at her skirt. Turning, she saw Desmond. His eyes were glued to the chicken carcase.

"My mum would boil that for soup."

Judy looked at him without affection.

"Not this one, she wouldn't. It's been left by gipsies and won't be very nice. It's going in this dustbin. What are you doing? Having a walk?"

Desmond's eyes turned to Nicholas.

"Great-grandad was put in a hole in the ground." Nicholas signalled to Judy to put the lid back on the dustbin. He took Desmond by the hand.

"I shouldn't worry about that, old man. I dare say your mother's told you about Paradise, hasn't she?" Desmond turned his face to the sky.

"Lightning came down once. It was thrown by God and burnt up a tree at Mr. Morris' farm."

Judy took Desmond's other hand.

"This is Mr. Parsons, Desmond. He asked you a question. He said, did your mother tell you about Paradise?"

Desmond, finding himself supported on each side, tried to swing.

"When I swing I'm like a bird, I can fly right away." Judy winked at Nicholas.

"I think that's a grand idea. Let's see how fast he can run, shall we?"

But Desmond was apparently enjoying himself. He clung firmly to them both.

"I'm going to show you something."

Nicholas looked down at him.

"Where?"

"I got something secret what nobody doesn't know."

Judy nodded at Nicholas.

"You see."

He nodded back at her.

"Let's see what the young man's secret is. I feel this is my day in getting to know the family. I'm coming up to the house. I want to meet Desmond's mother."

Desmond could apparently hear a conversation even if he could not join in one. He snatched his hands from them.

"I'm going to play. Nobody can't stop me."

They had reached the corner of the lane. Desmond skipped off singing to himself. In silence Judy and Nicholas watched him until he was out of sight, then Judy looked at Nicholas.

"What do you think?"

He shrugged his shoulders.

"I certainly shouldn't call him like other children. I think he's what used to be called a changeling. Do you suppose he'll tell his mother about the chicken?"

Judy laughed.

"I'm so glad you asked that. Shows you're getting the point of view of the subjugated people. Are you really coming to meet Clara?"

"I certainly am. The more I hear about Mrs. Roal the more she intrigues me."

Clara was on the lawn sewing. Even at so peaceful a task she looked alert and purposeful. She had chosen a hard green chair on which to sit, and even then did not relax. She sat upright, her fingers flying, her face intent. She raised her head as Judy and Nicholas came towards her. Judy introduced Nicholas.

"We made friends on the train coming down here," she explained. "He's in my factory. He's on experimental work."

Clara shook hands and told Nicholas where to find some deck-chairs. Nicholas fetched them and turned his to face Clara.

"I crashed in on your grandmother's picnic." Clara went on sewing.

"I'm sorry, I wish I'd known, I'd have cut some more sandwiches."

"It was all right," said Nicholas cheerfully. "We managed splendidly."

Clara glanced at Judy.

"Where're Grandmother and Aunt Rose?"

"Coming, I expect. Nick and I went for a little walk and we met Desmond."

Clara's hands paused at their sewing.

"Oh! What was he doing?"

Nicholas noted the pause and, though it did not show in his voice, there was sympathy in his eyes.

"Running around on his own business. I remember myself at that age, don't you? What terrifically important things one had to do. Does he go to school, Mrs. Roal?"

Clara obviously did not like discussing Desmond.

"No. He's an unusually highly strung child, brilliant in some things, backward in others. I think he's better educated alone." She laid down her work a moment and her voice took on a note of friendliness. "As you're a friend of Judy's, will you persuade her for me to get a new billet? This is rather a sad house, my grandfather died quite recently and I lost my husband in an air raid, it's not the place for a young girl."

Judy broke in.

"But I don't want to move, thank you very much. I'm happy here. Nick thinks your grandmother and Miss Rose are pets."

Again Clara's fingers hesitated at their work. Her voice was harder.

"But you do see what I mean, Mr. Parsons?"

Nicholas glanced at Judy. She made a face at him.

"Well, I'm afraid I don't know Judy well enough to interfere with her arrangements. This is a perfectly charming old house, and Mrs. and Miss Former seem very fond of her."

Clara sewed on steadily. When she spoke again it was in an entirely different tone.

"And how's she doing at the factory? It's curious work, I should think, after nursing." She did not wait for an answer but turned to Judy. "What kind of nursing did you do?"

Judy leant back in her chair and put her hands behind her head.

"Well, I started first helping in the holidays; we had evacuated children, nearly all with impetigo. I did chores. Nobody knows what chores can be until they've worked under what used to be the matron of a work-house. Later on, when I'd left school, I was promoted. I worked in the wards, we had quite a lot of real nursing to do there, pneumonia and broken limbs, you know what children are."

Clara was plainly interested.

"What exactly did you do? Just washed the patients, I suppose."

Judy sighed at her memories.

"There was absolutely nothing that I didn't wash, and, of course, I had some boiling to do too, all the instruments and syringes and things."

Clara gave Judy another interested glance.

"Did you give any actual treatment?"

"Oh, yes, I was doing almost everything at one time. Nurses are scarce, you know, and we had epidemics. Thank goodness I didn't kill anybody."

Nicholas laughed.

"That's a comfort. I was wondering whether we were going to unearth the fact that you'd come to work in the factory because of the slaughter you'd committed by giving the kids the wrong medicine."

Judy turned to him, her eyes twinkling.

"It's all very well for you to laugh, you'd be surprised what a flap I used to be in. Always thought I should put the temperature down wrong or give a solid meal to a light diet, or inject the wrong thing."

Clara had stopped sewing.

"Do you mean to say they trusted you with injections?"

"Well, some of the routine ones were simple to give. I was only joking when I said I could have given the wrong ones. I was heavily supervised, believe me. The girls on my group at the factory say things about our forewoman, they think she's strict, but nobody knows the meaning of the word strict who hasn't met my matron."

Nicholas had taken out his cigarette-case. He held it out casually to Clara, then paused. Clara had raised her head and was gazing at Judy, who, quite unconscious that she was being looked at, was staring at the sky. There was something he could not understand in Clara's expression, something he did not like. He leant towards her.

"Won't you have a cigarette?"

Mrs. Former and Miss Rose were flustered but pleased to see Nicholas on their lawn. Mr. Jones greeted him as an old friend.

"Well, isn't this nice!" said Mrs. Former in a fluttery voice. "Have you told Clara that we met?"

Nicholas had got out of his chair. He gently put Mrs. Former into it. He spoke clearly in her ear.

"I told her you kindly shared your picnic with me and that we managed splendidly."

"I do hope," Miss Rose broke in, "that you'll stay to tea, we could manage that, couldn't we, Clara?"

Clara got up.

"I'll go and put on the kettle. There isn't much, but if Mr. Parsons is not very hungry we can manage." She was turning to go when she saw Desmond coming in at the gate. She raised her voice. "Not out here, Desmond, in the kitchen. Mummy's just coming."

Desmond obviously paid no more attention to what his mother had to say than to other people. He came purposefully across the lawn, one hand behind his back. Clara moved towards him. As soon as he was within earshot Desmond raised his voice.

"Chicken soup, chicken soup."

Miss Rose, Judy and Nicholas exchanged furtive glances. Mrs. Former smiled vaguely.

"What's the child saying?"

Clara had hold of Desmond. She drew his hand from behind his back and took out of it the chicken carcase.

"That's dirty, Desmond, you shouldn't pick up old bones."

Desmond's face grew red. He was clearly annoyed at losing his carcase.

"She put it away in a tin. Like they put great-grandfather in the churchyard."

Judy felt it was time to intervene.

"Desmond found us putting it into a dustbin. We'd – that is, Nicholas and I – had found it on the road. Gipsies, I expect. We thought it ought to be salvaged."

Mrs. Former never could catch conversation that was not directed towards herself. She nodded at Miss Rose.

"Explain it was a present, dear."

Nicholas came over to Clara. He roared so that Mrs. Former would hear.

"That's why we said we managed marvellously. One should always bring gifts to a picnic, you know."

Clara turned in an annoyed way to Miss Rose.

"Why all this mystery? And how very wasteful to throw away the carcase. What a mercy the child had the sense to bring it home for soup. I'll put it on to boil now. You must all have been rather hungry to eat an entire bird. It would have been nice, if you could have saved a little, chicken is good for the child. Come along, Desmond."

Tea over, Nicholas and Judy decided to go to church. Judy put on a light coat and a hat and they strolled off.

"It's a very good thing," said Judy, "that I'm taking you to church. You've got a great deal on your conscience. Your gift to the picnic indeed!"

Nicholas did not answer that one. He walked along in silence till they came to the public road.

"I'm quite willing to agree that Mrs. Former and Miss Rose are dears, and I know you're not the sort to be pushed out of a billet to suit somebody else's convenience, all the same, I wish you'd get out of that house."

Judy stopped to have a look at some nuts to see if they were ripening.

"Well, I won't. I'm not a fool, I can see she wants to get rid of me, but she's not going to. I've a feeling that I'm a sort of protection to the old lady and Miss Rose, that if I wasn't there she really might starve them."

Nicholas' face was serious.

"I can't think what it is, but there's something I don't like. It's not just being mean, lots of people are that, there's something more to it. You know, she had some purpose in asking you all those questions about nursing."

"Nonsense, you're getting imaginative. Why on earth should that interest her?"

"I don't know, but it did. You were looking at the sky, but I was looking at her and she had the queerest expression."

"What sort?"

"Wish I knew, something I couldn't place, but something I didn't like."

Judy kicked at a stone that lay in her path.

"All right then, let's admit it. There's something about Clara Roal that neither of us like, but let's admit at the same time there's something about Judy Rest which is not easily frightened, and there's certainly something about Judy Rest which is not going to allow her to be frightened out of a house while two defenceless old women live in it. Now, let's drop the subject and let's hope we have one of those hymns about angel guards, for after this conversation I feel I need one."

CHAPTER V

THEY had switched on the loud speakers. Judy stopped humming and let her capstan turret swing to "Coming Home on a Wing and a Prayer". "How quickly one gets used to things," she thought. "Three weeks ago I couldn't believe I could hear the music over the din in here, and now I don't notice the din." She felt a touch on her arm and turned. The welfare supervisor was beside her. Except for a "getting on all right?" and a nod and a smile the welfare supervisor had not so far had any dealings with Judy. Now she was clearly paying a business call. She had some papers in one hand and a pencil obviously poised to write in the other.

"It's Judy Rest, isn't it?" Judy nodded. "I understand you want to change your billet."

A mass of words collected in Judy's mind ready to pour out, but she held them back. No good splurging all she thought about Clara to the welfare supervisor, who would not be interested and would merely think she was one of those girls who took unreasoning dislikes to people.

"No, I don't."

The welfare supervisor frowned at the paper in her hand.

"You don't! This report has come from your billet. It says that it is not suitable for you. Have you been complaining about anything?"

"No. I like it there."

The welfare supervisor looked worried.

"Have you done anything to upset the family?"

Judy shook her head.

"No."

The welfare supervisor was clearly puzzled. She was a nice woman with a youngish face under grey hair and a friendly smile. She had been summing Judy up and decided to take her into her confidence.

"It's a note I've had from your landlady." She opened a folded sheet of paper. "It says, 'Miss Judy Rest, whom you have billeted on this house, is not suited here. We also feel this house is not right for her and would be glad if you could arrange something else as soon as possible'."

"Fancy that!" said Judy. "Who signed that letter?"

"Mrs. Roal."

Judy smiled.

"Oh, her! Well, it's not her house, you know."

"Not? But it's with her I've fixed previous billets. And it's with her I communicated when a charge hand felt she should move. It was because of a death in the house."

"That's right. Mrs. White." Judy tapped Clara's letter. "I think she doesn't like billetees. She's the granddaughter by marriage and the only young person in the house, so it's all extra work for her, but she can't turn me out. The person who should have written if she wants me to be moved is Mrs. Former. It's her house."

"But isn't she very old and not able to do business?"

"Goodness, no! If you and I are one quarter as spry when we're that age we'll be fine. She's a little deaf and she's a diabetic, but she's very much all there, and very independent. Always injects her own insulin."

"You sound fond of her."

"I am and of her daughter, Miss Rose. She's another old pet."

"I see, and this Mrs. Roal, the grand-daughter by marriage, lives with them to look after them."

"Don't you believe it. To look after herself and her boy, Desmond. Between them Mrs. Former and Miss Rose could manage quite all right on their own, even with me thrown in."

The welfare supervisor's eyes were twinkling.

"I understand, my dear. By the way, my name is Mrs. Edwards. Now, what do you suggest I do? Write to Mrs. Former?"

"You might, so that you'll see I'm telling you the truth. I'll tell her it's coming."

"And Mrs. Roal?"

"Wait until you've heard from Mrs. Former. Then if she writes the sort of answer I think she will you can just tell Clara where she gets off. Do her good."

Mrs. Edwards was making a note on her pad. She paused and looked up, her face serious.

"If I might advise you, my child, go about this tactfully. You don't want to make an enemy, do you?" She clearly wanted to say more, then changed her mind. "Well, I'll go and write to Mrs. Former. I'll come and see you again when I hear from her."

Queer how that talk upset Judy. Of course she knew Clara did not want her in the house, but she had not thought she would go to such lengths to get rid of her. Why? Of course she made work, but not much. She ate, but then she brought her rations to the house. That the house was dull for her was Clara's story, but why should Clara care? She had no interest but Desmond. It looked as though she was up to something. But what? Was it money? "Wishing will make it so" sang a voice through the loud speaker. "I wish wishing would make me understand Clara," thought Judy. "Suppose she's sneaking a bit that she saves on the books, which more than likely she is, which would account for her being so mean, what am I going to do about it? Even suppose I knew she was parking a bit, she can't suppose I'd be able to stop her. I might be able to persuade Mrs. Former to go and see Mr. John, that lawyer of hers, but I doubt it. Besides, what possible reason can Clara have for thinking I'd interfere with her? Why should she fuss about me? I'm not the interfering sort."

You can't work a lathe and let your attention completely wander. Judy, moving some waste, brought one of her tools across her knuckles, and she had three quite deep cuts. She held her hand well away from her overall and felt for a handkerchief.

The charge hand came to her. She examined the cuts. "You'll have to go to the first aid, dear. It's in number eight bay. You feel all right to go alone?"

Judy twisted her bandage round her fingers.

"Of course. It's nothing. If I had some bandage I'd treat them myself."

There were two or three patients waiting for attention in the first-aid post, and only the nurse in charge and a V.A.D. to look after them.

"Sit down over there, dear." The nurse pointed to some chairs. "I won't be a minute."

Judy sat and studied the V.A.D. with a professional eye, wondering how she got on with the nurse, and how much real first-aiding she was allowed to do.

"I hate all this smell of disinfectant, don't you?"

Judy turned to the speaker, a big woman in her forties, with a determined but generous mouth and wrinkles of laughter round her eyes.

"I don't notice it. I was a V.A.D. myself before I came here."

The woman's face grew interested.

"You're not Miss Rest?"

"Yes, I am. Why?"

"I was wanting to meet you. You see, you're in the billet I was in. I'm Mrs. White."

The fragments that she knew about Mrs. White fell into a pattern in Judy's mind. She was a woman who liked things run her way. She disliked Clara; well, she wasn't alone in that. She must be fairly friendly with Nicholas for she had told him how the house gave her the creeps. Nicholas was the sort of person everybody liked and would talk to, but he was also the sort of person who could avoid, without appearing rude, being talked to when he did not want to be. Obviously, therefore, he had wanted to talk to Mrs. White, and that made Judy feel there must be something nice about Mrs. White. She smiled at her.

"How did you like our Clara?"

Mrs. White had a most expressive face. It now creased as if it was revolted by some appalling smell.

"She's a shocker, dear. Made my skin creep."

"You mean, because of the food?"

"Oh, no! She tried that on, but she didn't get far with that with me. Come on, I said, let's see me butter ration, put me jam in front of me, and if you can't do better than that with me meat ration I'll do the shopping meself, and I kept me points. I don't mind the expense, I said, but I won't starve. I'll lay out the points and see that I eat them."

Judy giggled.

"I wish I'd been a fly on the wall. But if it wasn't starvation why did she give you the creeps?"

Mrs. White looked round to see that nobody was listening. She dropped her voice to a whisper.

"It was when the old man died."

Judy's eyes widened.

"What happened then?"

"Gloat. That's the only word."

"But Mrs. Former said she looked after him so wonderfully."

"Too true. Couldn't have been more devoted. That's what made it so extra queer."

"How d'you mean?"

"Well, if you looked after somebody, wouldn't you get downed a bit if they didn't get on? You see, he wasn't really ill, only run down and needing a bit of care and a tonic."

"Didn't she mind?"

"No. I tell you it gave me the shudders. The night the old boy conked out she had a kind of triumph look. It wasn't nice at all. Of course, his going so suddenly was a shock to everybody, and I suppose that's how it took her, but it was queer somehow. Anyway, I couldn't get out quick enough. You should have seen me run to Mrs. Edwards! 'Out,' I said, 'out. Put me on a couple of chairs in the church if you've nothing else, but I've spent the last night I'm spending in Old House, Longbottom Lane'." She got up, for the nurse was looking at her. "You take my advice and move. There's something queer about that Clara. You mark my words."

Judy, with her fingers bandaged, came back to her machine. Shirley enquired after the cuts, but she did not give Judy time to answer.

"There's been an announcement. There's going to be a dance on Saturday. Special do with spot prizes and all sorts. It's part of that holidays-at-home stuff. You'll come, won't you?"

"How do they work? Do you have to bring a partner?" Shirley dug an elbow into Judy.

"Give over! As if everybody didn't know who you'll bring. But, as a matter of fact, you don't need to bring anyone. It's in and out of one pair of arms after another and, if you'll take my advice, don't wear your last pair of good shoes. Some people's dancing!"

"Does the whole works come?"

Shirley looked pitying.

"Not the office staff. You don't think they'd foul their lovely fingers touching the likes of us! No, dear, just the people who make the shells. Us, in fact."

Judy laughed. The incredible feeling of superiority which permeated the office staff was outside her understanding, but she knew it truly existed.

"What d'you wear?"

Shirley looked across at her machine on which the setter was working.

"A long frock if you have one because it always looks nicest, I think. I wear a long dress, but then I sing some of the numbers with the band. But anything you have does. You could come in trousers if you liked."

For the rest of the day Judy's mind kept turning to the dance. She had no doubt Nicholas would come. No doubt that he would dance with her, but a queer doubt of herself. What was this excitement at the thought of his arms round her? Was she getting sloppy about him? For goodness' sake, no. There had been plenty of other men who had liked her and she them, and they'd had a grand time at dances, but there'd been no slop. It was pretty stupid to be feeling like that alone, for there was nothing sloppy about Nicholas. He looked upon her as a friend and a sister. Pretty good laugh he'd have if he knew she was getting all of a do-da at the thought of dancing with him.

Judy was still deep in these thoughts at knock-off time, so she did not see Nicholas standing outside the factory gates until he spoke to her. She jumped and to her fury, for almost the first time in her life, flushed.

"Goodness, you startled me!"

He fell into step beside her.

"I came to ask you to have a drink."

"I'd adore one." She felt she must explain the flush. "I was thinking about clothes. There's a dance on Saturday."

"I know. I'm an M.C. part of the time, but the rest of the evening I can dance. You'll keep some for me?"

"Actually, except for our setter, you're the only man I really know, so I should think it's more a case of you keeping some for me."

He gave her one of his shy slow smiles.

"That's what you think. But I meet the men Home Guarding and you wouldn't believe what a sly dog I'm considered for knowing you. I was apparently considered a bit of a bookworm before, but since you came on the scene I'm supposed to be something of a lad. It's my ear into which go the worst of the stories, and when on the march we pass anything particularly dazzling in the way of a village beauty, they look at me and say, 'How's that? Up to your standard?'"

Judy remembered Shirley's dig.

"I believe it works both ways. I asked Shirley if one brought a partner and she told me not to put on an act." Nicholas nodded.

"I'm not sure of the local rules, but I think by Pinlock's standards we're what's known as walking out. That's the very early stages of what could blossom into a romance."

Judy felt her cheeks burning again. How difficult Nicholas was to compete with! He could say things like that and the words just meant what they appeared to. She must take a pull on herself and match his casual attitude.

Over shandies, for it was a ginless day at The Bull, Nicholas said:

"You've seen Mrs. White, I hear."

Judy was lighting a cigarette. She looked up in surprise.

"How on earth did you know that? Do you spend the whole day gossiping with the hands?"

"My dear girl, I'm Parsons for Punch. You know, the last knock is the one that counts. As a matter of fact, I—" he hesitated. "She sent a message she wanted to see me. The surgery had laid her off for the day." He touched Judy's bandages. "I heard about these and what was said."

"Yes?"

"I told Mrs. White I could do nothing with a stubborn creature. I said she had been warned."

"But what about? Mrs. White thought that Clara gloated when the old man died. Well, suppose she did? Suppose she was pleased? Suppose his death meant she had his money in her hands and could do more what she liked, what the hell's it got to do with me? My death wouldn't do her any good."

Nicholas played with his beer mug.

"It's just unpleasant. I, amongst others, don't like it."

Judy fixed her eyes firmly on his.

"Well, let's drop the argument. I'm not being stubborn or difficult, but I just think, if you'll let me sound a bit smug, the old lady and Miss Rose find me a prop and stay, and as long as that's so, I stop."

Nicholas nodded.

"I told Mrs. White you'd say that." He sipped his beer. "The week after next is August bank holiday. I have to go and see my mother. Care to come?"

Judy's heart somersaulted, but she managed to keep him from knowing.

"Is my journey really necessary?"

"I think so. With the works closed for three days Clara really could starve you. Will you come?"

Judy thought of his mother. Of her dead sons and what Nicholas must mean.

"It's nice of you; I think I won't. I imagine your mother rather counts on getting you to herself."

"As a matter of fact it's partly to give the old lady a kick that I asked you. When Dennis and Lionel were about the house crawled with pin-up girls."

Judy tipped back her beer.

"I wonder just what sort of pin-up girl I look. The sort with only stockings, or just a muff made of flowers?"

She could not get a rise out of him.

"I've told you before, 'the girl behind the gun'. Red hair, blue eyes and all the rest of it. Will you come?"

She leant across the table.

"Being serious for once, don't you think honestly she'd rather have you alone?"

He smiled, and getting up came round the table and tucked his hand under her arm and raised her out of her chair.

"If I thought that I wouldn't have asked you. I dote on my mother. And, apart from her, it suits me. You will stop on at that billet and I can't stop you; but you can't stop my protective eye on you. One cry of 'Nick, I'm starving!' and there I'll be with a tin of pilchards."

She laughed.

"Does that mean you'll never go away without me?"

He laughed with her.

"It does. Aren't you learning nicely?"

CHAPTER VI

MRS. Former and Miss Rose were as excited about Judy's dance as though they were going to it themselves. Judy had a yellow organdie frock, the result of being a bridesmaid to a fellow V.A.D. It was a pretty but, she had thought, almost useless dress, for yellow organdie with a bronze and orange twisted sash hardly seemed to have a place in the war. She had, in fact, brought it with her more with the idea of cutting up its slip for underclothes than with the intention of wearing it; but now that Shirley had assured her that a long frock would not be out of place, she was delighted that she owned such a garment, if only for the intense pleasure it gave to Mrs. Former and Miss Rose.

Miss Rose insisted on being in charge of the ironing and pressing.

"You give it to me, dear. Organdie has to look as fresh as fresh or it's nothing, I always say, and you haven't time to do it. You give it to me and I'll have it so you wouldn't know that it had ever been worn."

Mrs. Former smiled at the dress affectionately.

"When I was a young girl I had a silk gown in rather that style. It was a watered silk. I think there was a bunch of daisies somewhere. My uncle was a farmer in quite a big way and there used to be some sort of dance given for the farmers by the Hunt, that's where I wore it. I was wearing it the first time I met my husband." She stroked the organdie. "I do love to see young girls in pretty things. There are not nearly enough pretty things for young girls in this war." She stooped and lifted Mr. Jones on to her knee. "You must be a good boy and not rub up against Judy on Saturday." She turned to Judy. "He's a very sensitive dog, I believe he would actually grieve if he thought he had spoilt your dress."

The atmosphere of pleasure and goodwill surrounding Judy and her dance was spoilt by Clara. Clara's reactions Judy found baffling. If Clara, who was young and good-looking, had been bitter and perhaps a little jealous somebody else was going to have fun, when she was tied to the house by a child, it would have been entirely understandable, but although Clara was unpleasant, there was not a sign that it came from jealousy.

"Now, for goodness' sake, Aunt Rose, don't spend all day ironing that dress, because I know that's going to mean that you won't just heat the irons on the stove, but will plug in the electric iron, and that means waste."

"It doesn't cost very much," Miss Rose murmured.

One of Judy's tribulations was her inability to keep Mrs. Former and Miss Rose from putting their foot in it. She knew exactly what Clara was going to say before she said it.

"I sometimes wonder why we go to the expense of having a wireless in this house and taking a daily paper. Nobody seems to profit in the slightest by what they hear or read. If it wasn't for me no one in this house would pay the remotest attention to the fuel campaign." Judy broke in before Miss Rose had time to blunder further.

"Clara is absolutely right." She tucked her arm through Miss Rose's. "It's angelic of you to say you'll iron it, but it's got to be irons heated on the kitchen stove or nothing."

It seemed a week that was bound to make friction. On the Friday two things happened, both of which caused as much trouble as an incendiary bomb. Mrs. Edwards' letter arrived in the morning, but Mrs. Former was out with Mr. Jones and she so seldom got letters that the fact that there was one for her escaped her attention until the evening. Judy had just returned from work and had come in to have a word with the old lady. Miss Rose, hearing Judy's voice, came dashing out from the kitchen singing:

> "Truly Jerusalem name we that shore,
> Vision of peace, brings joy evermore."

"Is that you, dear? Come and look at your dress." It was then that Mrs. Former looked up at the mantelpiece and saw her envelope.

"Is that a letter, Judy dear? Who's it for?"

Judy saw the typed name and address and in a flash knew what the letter was about and at the same moment saw Clara standing in the doorway.

"It's for you, but it looks very dull, just a bill I should think."

The word bill brought Clara into the room.

"Really, Grandmother, don't you ever look at your letters, you know I always put them on the mantelpiece for you. That came this morning." She took the envelope from Judy and handed it to Mrs. Former, her face curiously flushed, her fingers trembling. "It can't be a bill, you can have absolutely nothing to spend money on. Nothing."

Mrs. Former was very easily cowed by Clara. Now she fumbled for her reading-glasses, keeping up what was to Judy a pitiful little running commentary.

"Of course not, dear, I haven't bought anything for quite a while. There was that tiny bag for Rose at Christmas, but you know about that, and I only put coppers in the collection, though I feel very badly about it, we have always given silver in this house. Oh, dear, where are my glasses? What a silly, clumsy old woman I'm becoming!" Suddenly she found the glasses, put them on her nose and, with a knitting-needle, opened the envelope. She pulled out a sheet of paper and guilelessly read the letter out loud. "Dear Mrs. Former, I have had a communication from your house about Miss Judy Rest, who is billeted with you. I understand from the letter that you do not think the house very convenient for taking in anyone, and that you also think the atmosphere a little depressing for a young girl. I have, however, spoken to Judy Rest, who tells me she is extremely happy with you. Would you let me know what you really feel about the matter? Yours sincerely, Lola Edwards." There was silence. Then Mrs. Former looked in a puzzled, pleading way at Judy. "What does this mean, dear?"

Judy was dead against a show-down, but she was not a person to turn from it when it had to be. She turned to Clara.

"Mrs. Edwards, our welfare supervisor, came to me and told me you thought I'd better make a change, that the house is not suitable for me, and I told her that I was happy, and it was Mrs. Former's house; she would have to decide whether I was to go or not."

Clara seemed quite unmoved by this disclosure.

"I suppose to you it does seem a matter for my grandmother," she raised her voice, "but I find the charge of a child and two elderly women, one of whom is becoming a little senile, more than I can cope with. If necessary I shall take steps to bring the law on my side." Mrs. Former heard every word of the last part of the sentence. She gave a scared cry.

"Judy!"

Judy ran to her and knelt down by her chair and put her arms round her.

"What nonsense, Clara! Mrs. Former's worth two of anybody else in this house, aren't you, darling? Senile indeed!"

Clara shrugged her shoulders and turned to the door, then she remembered what she had come about.

"Aunt Rose, have you moved that piece of steak?"

It was Miss Rose's turn to flush and tremble.

"No, oh, no indeed! It was on the shelf in the larder. I saw it there myself. I had brought a chair in to fetch a pot of jam off the top shelf and I remember looking down and saying to myself, 'What a splendid piece of steak!'"

Clara spoke loudly and distinctly.

"Did you put the chair back in the kitchen? And did you shut the larder door?"

Miss Rose trembled like an ill-set jelly.

"Well, dear, not quite at once because I ran up to fetch Judy's sash. The stove was hot, you know, and I was ironing this afternoon, but I remembered the very moment I came down."

Clara looked at Mrs. Former.

"Where is Mr. Jones?"

Mrs. Former, resting her hand on Judy's shoulder, lifted herself out of her chair.

"He was here a moment ago, dear. He's been with me the entire day. Perhaps the dear boy has stepped out into the garden. I'll go and see."

She pressed past Clara and hurried out into the hall. Miss Rose followed her twittering, "Oh, dear, I'm sure it wasn't Mr. Jones. I hope it wasn't Mr. Jones." Judy prayed hard mentally, but without much faith, "Oh, God, don't let Mr. Jones have taken it." In the passage all doubts were resolved. The dining-room door was open and Mr. Jones, unaccustomed to such heavy feeding, was getting rid of the steak on the dining-room carpet.

Judy put an arm round Mrs. Former because she felt the old lady was scared, as well she might be, for Clara at that moment was enough to scare anybody. A meat ration was, of course, a thing of value and Mr. Jones' crime no mean one, and his present exhibition depressing, to put it mildly, but even so, surely, thought Judy, even a year's rations could not be worth the scene that followed. Words poured out of Clara's mouth like water out of a tap, not even sensible words, but a jumble about keeping dogs while children starved, and having no thought for the future, playing ducks and drakes with money of which you were only a trustee, and, finally, with tears in her eyes:

"None of you know or care how cruel life can be." Then, as if unable to bear the sight of any of them, she dashed blindly into the kitchen.

Miss Rose moaning, "First a shovel and some newspaper and then a wet towel," ran after Clara.

Judy led the old lady back into the sitting-room. She sat down beside her and stroked her hand, then smiled up at the scared old face.

"Don't look so serious, darling. If all of us make do with a bit of potato for supper to-night we've atoned for Mr. Jones' crime." She giggled. "It's funny really, you know. He is the most awfully tactless dog, let's face it. If only he'd been sick in the garden nobody could absolutely prove what he'd done."

Mrs. Former clutched at Judy's hand.

"I'm so frightened, dear, you know, she's spoken before about getting rid of him. You know, Judy dear, I should have no wish to live without Mr. Jones, he is such a companion."

Judy tried to make the old lady feel her warmth and affection. "Of course he is, and nobody's going to hurt the old pet."

Mrs. Former hugged Judy's hand.

"You've no idea what a comfort you are to myself and Rose, dear. I do so look forward to your comings and goings, and the little excitements in your life. It may seem fanciful, but I have sometimes imagined that the sun is not so bright since my husband died, but now see it through your eyes and I know that's pure imagination. You won't let Clara drive you from the house, will you, dear? Please."

Judy flung her arms round the old lady and kissed her. "Of course I won't. I'll stay with you as long as I work in the factory, and that's a promise."

The dance was held in the factory canteen. For the occasion the walls were hung with a strange mixture of the flags of the Allies and some artificial mimosa. On the stage was the works' band wearing funny cardboard hats, and in the case of the saxophonist a red nose. These humorous additions were to show that this was a gay occasion, for the band also functioned at special war-savings drives, an occasional service and about twice a week in the canteen. Nicholas, with a badge marked M.C. in his buttonhole, was standing in the middle of the room smiling shyly at everyone. His face lit up as he saw Judy. He hurried towards her and looked at her frock.

> "And then my heart with pleasure fills
> And dances with the daffodils."

"One of my jobs as M.C. is to prevent girls sitting against the wall. So the moment you came in I thought to myself, 'Do the duty nearest, make poor Judy feel at home'."

Judy's eyes twinkled.

"How good of you. What are you going to do about me?"

Nicholas looked round. There were quite a lot of male eyes fixed on them both.

"It's going to be terribly difficult, but I'll do my best." He steered Judy towards a group of men. "Do you all know Miss Judy Rest?"

It was an hour later before Nicholas' turn as M.C. came to an end, but it was half an hour after that before he managed to get Judy for a dance.

"I do think," he said as he put his arm round her, "you might have been kinder to an old friend."

Judy had waited for this minute all the evening and had no wish now that it had come to spoil it with conversation. It was nice to have Nicholas so close to her. She had thought perhaps that his studious aloof air would be carried into his dancing, but not at all. The arm that held her gripped her firmly, almost possessively.

"I didn't want to spoil your evening," she explained. "I know what a worry we wallflowers are to you members of the committee."

It was a waltz that was being played. It was odd, Judy thought, how quite suddenly, instead of being part of an enormous, chattering crowd they had become just two people shut in, as it were, by the music. They came opposite the platform. Shirley was standing by the microphone. She grinned at them and began to sing:

"Daisy, Daisy, give me your answer do,
I'm half crazy all for the love of you."

Nicholas tightened his grip on Judy and joined in the singing.

"We won't have a stylish marriage,
For we can't afford a carriage,
But you'll look sweet upon the seat . . ."

He broke off. "Bit of an awkward walk from your billet in that long frock, wasn't it?"

"You ought to have seen me! It was pinned up by Miss Rose, and I carried my shoes under my arm, very like stepping out to a party in Grandmother's day, I shouldn't wonder."

"What's our Clara say about you coming to a party?" His words brought back the unpleasantness of yesterday. She frowned.

"Oh, she doesn't mind my going to a party, but she doesn't like me. She grudged Miss Rose wasting her time ironing my frock, and, most unluckily, the letter from Mrs. Edwards about the billet was read out loud by the old lady, and, to cap it all, Mr. Jones not only stole the meat ration but returned it on the dining-room carpet. The subjugated races are particularly subjugated to-day."

The waltz was coming to an end. Nicholas stood beside her.

"I know I've got several more dances with you, but I'd like to stake a claim now on seeing you home, may I? I could carry your shoes."

Judy had counted on his asking her that. It would be nice sauntering along with him in the dark, but there was no glimpse of her feelings in her voice.

"That's extremely good of you, Mr. Nicholas Alexander Gordon Parsons. Miss Judy Rest will be charmed."

It was a perfect night for a walk. The sky glittered with stars, there was a waxing moon which threw great black shadows and gave an air of mystery to the most ordinary buildings. At first Nicholas and Judy were part of the stream of couples going home, then suddenly they were alone in the lane. There was nothing but an occasional bird and the rustle of leaves and grasses in the light wind, and the sharp smell of late July flowers.

"I heard from my mother to-day," said Nicholas. "She's no end pleased that I'm bringing you down. She says that she'll like you if you're a friend of mine, but she does hope that you don't wear glasses and want to spend the days reading Greek." He took Judy's arm. "You don't want to read Greek, do you, sweet?"

Judy held her breath. He had called her "sweet" and said it in a special way, not just casually, but as if it was a word that he meant. Should she answer him in the same mood? Should she let this walk slip them into a sentimental, perhaps a little romantic, mood? Then caution stopped her. Any man might call a girl "sweet" at the end of a dance when she was looking nice in a party frock; it didn't mean that he felt any differently about her than when he saw her in her works overall. She knew in the back of her mind that she had got a good deal of serious thinking ahead of her, that she was getting a great deal fonder of Nicholas than was sensible, that she might, if she was not careful, run the risk of being stupidly hurt. Not that she was afraid of being hurt when there was purpose in it, but there was no purpose in getting to count on intimacy and friendship and something more than friendship when you knew you had no earthly reason to rely on getting it back. Nicholas had been thrown into a world to which he did not belong, thrown into a little village pub which had nothing in it of home, he was lonely and wanted distraction. She would be a poor silly fool if she let this need of his for companionship and distraction lead her into thinking that he wanted anything more.

"Talking of sweet," she said cheerfully, "don't you think Shirley an awful duck? It's curious, whatever dreary job you take up nice people like Shirley crop up that you would never have met in the ordinary way."

He looked at her with one of his more amused expressions.

"Knowing you, Judy, is remarkably like knowing a bit of quicksilver. You are a one for slipping about, aren't you?"

"That's right," Judy agreed, "the elusive type. It's supposed to be a very successful way of getting through life. Didn't you know?"

They had reached the gate into the private road. Nicholas opened it. It made a dismal squeak.

"Even on a night like this the entrance to your home seems to me particularly repulsive. I wonder why Mr. Former thought fit to bury himself in a mass of trees."

"I don't think he did. I think he was just awfully happy with his Mollikins – that's what he called Mrs. Former; and then, you know, he used to have some sick animals that he looked after, dogs mostly. I suppose they barked a bit and it was better not to have too many near neighbours."

"Where'd he keep the animals?"

"Round at the back. The kennels are being pulled down now. The wood is useful, you know, to repair the hen-houses and so on. I've got to go in at the back door anyway, I'll show you."

Because the evening was coming to an end Judy stopped talking. There was no harm in loving this arm-in-arm stroll. Nicholas would not know how much she was enjoying it. As if he sensed her mood, Nicholas too fell silent. They walked together softly up the path and round the side of the house. Judy led Nicholas across the yard where several dog-kennels stood.

"You see. It always makes me feel a bit gloomy look-ing at them. Mr. Former was awfully fond of animals, and somehow the dog-kennels seem sad without him."

Nicholas nodded.

"Useful wood though, and some nice bits of wire. Very hard to come by these days." He took out his torch and ran the light up and down the side of one of the kennels. "He believed in good workmanship." He stopped short. "Judy, look, isn't that Mr. Jones?"

Judy peered between the kennels. It was Mr. Jones. He lay unnaturally stiffly. Nicholas knelt down and ran his hands over the dog. Before he could speak Judy knew what he was going to say. Mr. Jones was dead.

CHAPTER VII

NICHOLAS strained forward between a soldier and an A.T.S. and managed to get his mouth near enough to Judy's ear to be heard.

"Splendid, life in a sardine-tin, isn't it?"

Judy was standing in a curve to make room for a stout woman who was sitting on her suit-case.

"This'll teach me to take journeys that aren't really necessary."

"After the next change there's a little local train. It's almost sure to be empty."

"You said that when we changed at Bristol and when we changed at Swindon, and after that awful wait at Reading, my morale is slipping."

"All the same it's true. It's a local train built like a bus and if all the inhabitants travelled on it at once there'd probably be room. There aren't many people in my village."

Judy sighed.

"Not many people. At the present moment I feel those are the most beautiful words ever spoken."

The soldier and the girl in the A.T.S. began talking and Nicholas withdrew to prop up his small bit of the corridor. Judy could just see him. He looked, she thought, remarkably fresh and unmoved, his flannel suit, what she could see of it, seemed uncrushed. He did not look dirty, his hair was still tidy. He looked tired, but then he very easily looked that. He was fine drawn and any exertion told on him. It was pretty mean, she thought, that he should be looking reasonably tidy, it could not possibly matter to him going home whether he looked tidy or not, and goodness knows what a mess she must be looking by now. She had so hoped to look well to greet his mother. She had put on a dark silk frock to travel in which had a light-weight coat to go with it. They were old, of course, but still good and did not show the dirt, but no frock could have stood up to to-day's journey. She hoped Nicholas was right about the next change, she was so tightly wedged she could not get at her handbag to do anything about her makeup and her hair must be looking a sight. Not that from what Nicholas had said his mother was the sort to be fussy about appearances, she did not like glasses and Greek, but she did not expect the ultra smart. Though quite likely Nicholas was wrong; men misjudged their mothers so terribly, especially they misjudged their mothers when it came to guessing the type of girl they would like their sons to bring home for visits. Or did no mother ever feel enthusiastic about her son's friends and acquaintances? She had not had actual experience herself, but she knew what happened to her friends, and the anxious thought they gave to meeting their various men's mothers, and she had heard snippets of conversation they repeated after they had met them, so many of which were not very kind. Judy was unwilling to accept it, but at the back of her mind she knew that she was considering Lady Parsons in just the way that her friends thought of the mothers of their men acquaintances. What she should wear, what she should say, what sort of impression she was going to make. "Stupid of me," she thought angrily. "It's no good trying to be any different to what I am, so it's much better to act naturally from the start," and then, as an afterthought, "I only wish I thought I would."

The train was slowing down. Nicholas gave her a look and raised his voice.

"This is our junction, in three-quarters of an hour we'll be home."

The slow local, shaped, as Nicholas had said, like a bus, was in and only partially full Nicholas and Judy sank thankfully down on one of the long seats which ran the whole length of the carriage. Judy opened her handbag.

"Isn't this gorgeous! Room to move my elbows and even to take a deep breath. Of course I quite realize one shouldn't expect these luxuries in war-time, but you can't help enjoying a little treat when it comes your way."

Nicholas opened his cigarette-case.

"We shall be able to smoke without burning our next-door neighbours. Sorry it's been such a foul journey. Are you regretting you started?"

She was making up her lips, but she managed to make a face at him.

"Idiot, of course not! Though, as a matter of fact, you very nearly got a telephone message this morning to say I couldn't come."

"No! Why?"

"The old lady; you know she hasn't been well since Mr. Jones died, and last night she was rather pathetic, crying and saying she hoped she would be there when I came back. It's nonsense, of course, she's had the doctor, it's only sort of shock. Clara's being marvellous, I must say. She seems to have forgotten to be mean for a change and keeps making up little dishes to tempt the old girl."

Nicholas lit his cigarette.

"You don't sound as if you really thought her marvellous."

Judy put away her lipstick and took out her comb.

"Isn't it awful of me? But, you know, I never can get over the feeling that Clara had a hand in finishing off Mr. Jones. There's not the slightest ground for it. She couldn't have been kinder or more sympathetic, it's just my suspicious nature, I suppose."

"And mine."

She swung round to him.

"Did you think that too? You never said anything."

"I did more than think. I had a post-mortem held on the poor old boy."

Judy gasped.

"But you couldn't. He was buried the evening after we found him and I was present at his funeral, and stayed up till goodness knows what hour of the night covering his grave with little grass clods."

Nicholas nodded.

"And building up a cairn as a tombstone, and a lot of trouble you gave me, for after midnight I pulled the whole thing down and took the old boy out and put some stones in his place and built his grave up again."

"Do you mean to tell me," said Judy severely, "that I'm ordering some extremely expensive bulbs to decorate the grave of a pile of stones?"

He nodded.

Judy dropped her voice.

"What did you find out at the post-mortem?"

"Nothing. Just Anno Domini. He seemed to have nothing much the matter with him. His heart just stopped beating."

"You don't sound very convinced about it."

"Well, there was nothing in the post-mortem to make me feel that way. It was just an odd circumstance, I suppose. I mean his death coming as it did straight on top of her being angry about his stealing the meat, but the vet did say he couldn't see why on earth he should die. You see, there was no history of a weak heart. He seems to have been, from what Mrs. Former said, a remarkably brisk old boy for his age." He flicked his ash on to the floor. "I hate that damn house and all there is about it, or rather I detest that woman Roal. All my life I have had quick reactions to people, it's a thing that you're born with. I should hate to tell you what my reactions are to Clara."

Judy held out her hand for a cigarette.

"I don't like her, but I can't help being sorry for her. You know, she's under no real illusions about that boy of hers. Clara's no fool. How awful it must be to have a child like that! All right now that he's little, she can get away with pretending he's unusual and all the rest of it, but one day he'll be a man. He really is rather like what you called him, a changeling, but that won't be so funny when he's grown up. Poor Clara, I shouldn't wonder if she lies awake at night scared of something happening to her and wondering who'll take care of Desmond."

Nicholas gave her one of his nicest smiles.

"You think a lot, don't you?"

Lady Parsons was standing on the platform. She was wearing her W.V.S. uniform and had two cocker spaniels on leads. She started to talk as Judy and Nicholas got out of the train.

"The car's gone again, Nick; it's the back axle this time and the man at the garage says that he shouldn't think that he'll get it mended this war. I explained I must have it for my work, but he seemed to think I'd have to buy another car. Did you ever hear such nonsense! But I had a bit of luck about to-day. There's no funeral, and I have hired that old black Wolseley that the undertaker uses to carry the mourners."

Nicholas drew Judy forward.

"This is Judy, Mother."

Lady Parsons beamed.

"How do you do, dear? How nice you look. Such a comfort! Nicholas never does bring girls home, but if he did I was afraid he'd bring the sort that look terribly clever."

Nicholas bent down to pat the dogs.

"That's right, Mother, put your foot in it right away. Tell Judy she looks a moron."

"Judy knows just what I mean," said Lady Parsons firmly. "I don't mind how clever a woman is as long as she makes up her face and doesn't do her hair peculiarly." She pointed to her dogs. "These are Scylla and Charybdis, dear. I've had them since they were puppies. My son, Lionel, christened them. Either Scylla or Charybdis, I never can remember which, was a whirlpool, and the other was a rock. Lionel knew that one of the puppies was a whirlpool, but he hoped the second would grow into a rock. Nothing of the sort ever happened, of course, it never does with puppies, does it? Now, do come on, dears. The man who's driving the car doesn't like being out late; you see, he's used to funerals and they're over in decent time."

Lady Parsons owned a manor-house. A long, tree-shaded drive led to what must have been a formal garden behind which lay the house. Both the house and garden looked badly in need of attention. One of the lawns had been allowed to grow for hay and the borders of flowers were in need of stakes and twine. Nothing could spoil the beauty of the house, which was late Queen Anne, but the paint was peeling off the window-frames and there was attention needed to the gutterings.

Nicholas went ahead carrying Judy's and his own bags into the house.

"I expect you're tired, dear, and you would like to go in too," Lady Parsons suggested, "but if not, it's lovely on the lawn, and I'm actually going to be able to offer you a drink. The inn in the village is built on my property, and Smithers, the landlord, is a very old friend, and when he heard Nick was coming home and bringing you, he said, 'You can trust me to raise something, my lady,' and the something proved to be one bottle of whisky and one bottle of gin. It's really very good of him. I must remember to give him a pot of honey if my bees do any good this year."

"It's a lovely house."

"Yes, but abominably big. There's only myself and Dibble. Dibble was my personal maid before the war, but now she does everything. Up till the war was declared Dibble went on from year to year being thirty-nine, and then suddenly, when registration started, she came to me one morning and laid her birth certificate on my desk and there she was fifty-two. Of course I said nothing about the thirty-nine, I was too thankful. I just said, 'Isn't that splendid, Dibble!' and she said, 'Yes, my lady,' and we've never mentioned it since."

Judy ran her eyes over the numerous windows.

"Do you mean to say that Dibble does the whole of this house?"

Lady Parsons moved off along her garden path. She stared at the flowers as if she found that easier than studying her windows.

"Oh, no, dear, we just use her bedroom and mine, and what used to be the breakfast-room and the kitchen, and, of course, the bathroom. Everything else is closed. To-day, of course, we've opened the spare bedroom for you and the little dressing-room for Nick. Nick's bedroom was up there" – she jerked her head towards the upper windows without looking up. "It was a wing we kept for the boys; it's completely closed now and I shan't be opening it again."

Judy looked up at what had been the boys' wing. How empty the house must feel! Lady Parsons had probably lived there all her married life and she must have seen her boys at all ages peering out. With Nicholas away poor Lady Parsons and Dibble must find this a house of ghosts.

It almost seemed as if Judy had a ready-made niche in Nicholas' home. Scylla and Charybdis accepted her right away as part of the house. Dibble, who was very superior and not given to taking quick likings, told Nicholas that Miss Rest seemed to be a capable girl and she couldn't say otherwise, which, for Dibble, as Nicholas told Judy, was very high praise. Lady Parsons clearly liked her, for she took her into her confidence about her work, taking it for granted she would be interested, which was a high compliment.

"You see, dear, I'm the County Organizer. I don't mind any work that I have to do. I don't mind spending hours tracking down palliasse cases in answer to an SOS from Region, I enjoy second-hand clothes, I'm quite willing to care passionately about basic training, but I do hate little fusses. And, of course, you can't be in charge of any set of people, men or women, and not have little fusses. I remember my husband telling me in the last war that when his men had been through a really terrible time and came out reduced almost to half, the only complaint they had to make was about jam. My women work magnificently, with a selfless devotion which is quite lovely to watch, but when I go to see them they tell me some long story about a temporary oven which somebody ought to have built for an exercise and didn't, or about the poor quality of the knitting wool. It is quite understandable, of course. These things are to us what wrong jam is to the soldier, little complaints are natural, I suppose, but I was always one who preferred trying to look at the stars, if you follow me."

Nicholas obviously adored his home. He took Judy over all that could be covered in two days, and little by little, without being aware of it, he showed her his own childhood. The two strong energetic brothers and the frail Nicholas trying to keep up with them. "I tried so hard to jump that brook when I was eight because Lionel and Dennis had managed it, but I couldn't. I'd fallen in eighteen times before I was lucky, and I was in permanent disgrace. I managed it though just before my ninth birthday."

"Lionel and Dennis ran a telegraph service between those trees. I used to bounce about at the bottom absolutely stamping with rage because however high I jumped the lowest branch was right above my head. I was a very slow grower, then one day I thought of bringing down a chair. You should have seen Lionel's face when I popped up beside him."

"He used to have a practice-net down there, we had a coach in the summer holidays for Lionel and Dennis. He was supposed to keep an eye on me too, but I was never any good and he couldn't be bothered. Mother was marvellous; of course she was frightfully proud of Dennis and Lionel, you know, games captains and all that, but she never thought it mattered about me, and when we had cricket matches here she used to say, 'Thank goodness you aren't developing into a left-hand bat or anything startling. I do like having one of you to help me hand round'."

On Monday afternoon they had to leave. Nicholas was inside gossiping with Dibble. Lady Parsons led Judy on to the lawn and walked her up and down.

"It's very nice for Nicholas that you've come to work at his factory. He knows, of course, that he's doing useful work and that he won't be released to do anything else, but it's not easy for him. I have frequently to remind him what a miserable soldier he'd make. He would, you know, he'd always break down, he's delicate, and I understand he's important where he is, but, of course, men do feel it so when they aren't in danger and other people are."

Judy pictured the grass-covered mound under which Nicholas worked and the blast-proof wall round it as an extra precaution. Clever of him not to have let his mother know.

"It's marvellous for me," she said gently. "I'd be pretty lonely if he wasn't there. He's a very amusing companion."

"I expect you've noticed the difficulty he has in speaking of things that affect him closely."

Judy thought over her various talks with Nicholas. He had not said much about his private life or his affairs, but there was nothing unusual in that.

"No, I hadn't."

Lady Parsons stopped and patted Judy's arm.

"Well, he is very slow, dear. You remember that and help him out if he seems to you to be particularly inarticulate about anything!"

Judy looked up.

"What sort of things?"

"Well, I can't think of anything specific at the moment. It was really of the future I was thinking. He may want to talk to you about things, and when he does, don't forget what I have said."

Judy searched Lady Parsons' face. What did she mean? Was there something odd in Nicholas' life? Or was Lady Parsons trying to say that if Nicholas should ever show signs of caring for her – Judy broke off her thoughts there. It was nice if she was thinking that. If only she could hear Nicholas' conversations with her, how very far away they were from anything of that sort. However, it was pretty good to feel that his mother approved.

"I won't forget if ever he shows signs of becoming confidential, but he hasn't yet."

"He will," said Lady Parsons. "I feel sure he will." Nicholas came out of the house carrying his and Judy's bags.

"What are you two gossiping about?"

Casually Lady Parsons replied.

"I was telling Judy about my work for the W.V.S."

CHAPTER VIII

SHIRLEY, on the way to the canteen, tucked her arm through Judy's.

"Have a good time?"

Judy gave her an affectionate dig with her elbow.

"You know, you're wasted on this factory, you ought to be a policewoman. Nothing goes on that you don't know about, does it?"

Shirley moved her arm to Judy's shoulder and gave her a hug.

"If you think anybody catches the train from this station escorted by a man and the rest of us girls don't know about it, you're more of a fool than you look. But when it comes to you, who've set every girl in a jitter since the factory dance in case you nip off with one of their boys, you just can't take a step without us all knowing about it. A sort of running commentary went round Pinlock. 'Judy Rest is coming down the road with her suit-case.' 'Judy Rest has called in at The Bull. She's picked up Mr. Parsons. They've gone to the station,' and after that, of course, we just said oo-er!'"

"Just to satisfy your curiosity and not because I care a damn what any of you think I do with my week-ends, I stayed with his mother."

Shirley's eyes grew round with interest.

"No! What's she like? Very posh and la-di-da, I suppose."

Judy pictured Lady Parsons in her mind's eye.

"The least posh and la-di-da, in the sense you mean, person in the world I should think. She wears old clothes, I don't think she cares at all what anybody thinks about her. She's lost two sons in this war and minds all the time and never says a word about it. In fact, a perfect darling."

"She all right to you?"

"Couldn't have been more enchanting. She wasn't a bit like you'd think she'd be to some strange girl. I mean, you'd think she'd be a bit looking me over and all that."

Shirley giggled.

"I dare say she thought there was no need with a lifetime of doing that ahead of her."

They were in the canteen. They had to take their place in the queue so Judy had no chance to answer, for which she was grateful. Funny the way people would take it for granted that there was something more than friendship between herself and Nicholas.

Shirley and Judy sat down facing each other. Shirley, though she was eating hard, had a good look at Judy.

"Doesn't seem to have done you much good, your holiday. You look on the pale side. But then, I suppose it's a long journey."

"It's a beast, though I don't think that's why I'm looking pale, if I am. I came back to such a fuss, and I hate fusses."

"What's happened?"

Judy laid down her knife and fork.

"The old lady hasn't been well. It seems that while I was away she tripped in the garden, and though she wasn't much hurt Clara sent for the doctor, and the doctor had a talk with Miss Rose —that's Mrs. Former's daughter that I told you about, and he told Miss Rose the old lady was breaking up and ought to be looked after rather more, and amongst other things that she ought not to be allowed to give herself her own insulin injections. She might give herself too much or too little one day, and Clara's to give it to her."

"Fancy giving yourself an injection! I'd hate to."

"Insulin patients very often do look after themselves," Judy explained. "And Mrs. Former's a wonderfully independent old lady, hates to think she needs any help physically."

"Still, I suppose if the doctor's talked to Miss Former about it she'll talk the old lady into it, won't she?"

"Though she wouldn't admit it for worlds, the old lady doesn't like her granddaughter; she admires her and knows she's competent, and she's forced to admit that she's most frightfully good to her, but she hates the thought of being dependent on her. I'm fond of the old dear and I hate to see her in a state, but, of course, she'll have to give in in the end, now that the doctor's insisted, though, mind you, I can't think why he did, the old girl couldn't be more competent."

"If the old lady can't give herself an injection and doesn't like that Clara doing it, why don't you do it? You were trained in a hospital, weren't you? Is it difficult to give an injection?"

Judy's face lit up.

"Of course it isn't. How stupid of me not to think of it for myself; it's an awfully good idea, settle all the bother I expect. Between you and me, though I can give it, I shan't, I'll just stand beside the old lady and see she gives herself the right dose."

Judy tried out Shirley's suggestion as soon as she got in that evening. On the doctor's orders the old lady was having a day or two in bed. Her face lit up as Judy came in.

"There you are, dear! I was hoping you would find time to come up and see me. Doctor Mead is a very old friend and I'm certain would not keep me in bed unless he thought it necessary, and I don't like to offend him by getting up when he said I was to stay in bed, but, you know, Judy dear, there's nothing whatsoever the matter with me. You see, the trouble is that Clara fusses. On Sunday I tripped over a bit of string that was lying about; it had got caught up somehow on to a branch or something, and I would have had a very nasty fall, but fortunately I just saved myself and came down on my hands and knees, but by bad luck Clara was out collecting firewood and she saw me, but she couldn't find the string that I tripped over, though I know it was there because I felt it, and she insisted I had a giddy fit and sent for Doctor Mead, and I think must have seen him first and had a talk with him, because you know he is anything but an alarmist, but he treated me, dear, just like a child. Really, I could have slapped him. Then, to crown it all, the next day he told Rose that she was to take away my hypodermic and Clara was to give it to me. Of course I refused and made Rose go back and see him about it. Doctor Mead came up himself last night and gave me my injection, but he said I must let Clara do it to-night. Such nonsense!"

Judy took one of the old lady's hands and patted it. "That's what I came to see you about. I quite see that if the doctor's got it into his head that you ought not to be giving yourself a hypodermic that he won't let you, but I've got a suggestion to make. How would it be if I gave it? Not really, you know, because all I shall do is to see you give it to yourself. I'm perfectly used to them in hospital, and I'll see you don't have a giddy fit while you're putting the needle in."

She laughed as she said giddy fit.

Mrs. Former beamed at her.

"You do see it's nonsense, dear, I knew you would. But I think that's a perfectly splendid idea. It's very naughty of me, but I do dislike feeling dependent on Clara. I feel once she starts giving me injections she may go on doing it, and the next thing we know is that she's treating me like a baby." She gave Judy a conspiratorial twinkle. "Run along now, dear, and tell her that we've arranged everything."

Judy went to the kitchen quite thinking she would get thanks. Clara had more than enough to do, goodness knew, for the old lady now that she was in bed, and she would probably be only too thankful to have something taken off her hands. In the kitchen Clara was working at the stove, Desmond was standing at the window slapping vaguely at flies on the pane, and Miss Rose was out in the scullery singing at the top of her voice:

> "O happy band of pilgrims
> Look upward to the skies."

It was always understood that Clara reigned in the kitchen though Miss Rose pottered in and out. Judy never went in without asking permission. She stood now in the doorway.

"Can I come in, Clara?"

Judy's voice evidently penetrated Miss Rose's singing and she broke off in the middle of a line and came hurrying into the kitchen.

"Ah, there you are back, Judy dear. Would you go up and see Mother, she'd love to have a talk with you."

"I've been," Judy explained, "and that's what I've come to see Clara about." She turned to Clara. "You know what a fuss she's in about you giving her her insulin – well, it seems she wouldn't mind if I did it. I suppose it's because . . ." she broke off, staring at Clara.

Clara was at all times rather pale, but now she turned quite white, and the expression in her eyes, which were fixed on Judy, was intense, out of all proportion to the words that were being said. She spoke as she had on the day when Mr. Jones stole the meat ration. Words poured out of her mouth in a meaningless jabber. Why should she be insulted when she was perfectly capable of giving an injection, as the doctor well knew? Why did Judy always try to interfere? Life was difficult enough with a senile woman in the house without Judy making difficulties. It wasn't right that time should be taken from bringing up a sensitive little boy in order to keep old people going.

Judy felt quite stunned by the flow of words. What in the name of wonder was there to fuss about? As soon as Clara paused for breath, she broke in.

"But, Clara, if the old lady wants it, what's the objection? After all, I was trained in hospital."

Clara came to the edge of the kitchen table and beat on it with her fist.

"I knew that was coming. Throwing up your hospital training in my teeth, but let me tell you I was trained too. My husband sent me for classes. There's a lot of odd jobs you have to do in chemist's shops."

Judy did not know what to say. She was completely in the dark as to what had caused this outbreak. It was no good saying that Clara was unbalanced, even if she was and if she was going to be terribly upset about this injection business, nothing could alter what the old lady wanted, and, after all, the old lady was the patient.

Desmond gave her time to think. He suddenly wandered over to the table holding a dead fly between his fingers.

"I killed him. I killed a mouse once, stamping on it."

If there was one thing that Judy was sure of it was her violent revulsion to Desmond.

"Poor mouse," she said severely, before she had time to remember that Clara was present.

Clara gave Desmond a push.

"Go out into the garden, dear."

"The old wind has got tied up in our chimney, he's moaning and groaning."

Clara took the child by the hand.

"Go outside, dear."

She shut the back door, taking quite a time over it. When she came back to the table Judy was relieved to see that she looked more normal. She had been cooking when Judy came in, and she now went back to the stove. She spoke with her face over a saucepan.

"Sorry if I lost my temper, but life seems to be just one thing on top of another. I'll have a talk to the doctor to-morrow. If he says you can give the injections then I won't say any more about it, for to-night he's ordered a bit of a sedative, and I'm giving it her in some soup, and by the time I come up to settle her off she'll be too drowsy to care who puts the injection in, but as she's taken a fancy to you you can come up with me and sit with her while I do it."

It was still light when Judy and Clara went up to put the old lady to bed, that queer, unreal light of a summer evening. The sedative had done its work. Mrs. Former was not asleep, but she was too drowsy to say much, and contentedly let Judy and Clara make the bed and wash her and settle her for the night. On a tray on the window-ledge was the insulin. The syringe and its needle were lying in a jar on a bed of cotton wool soaked in surgical spirit. Clara, in an experienced way, picked the parts out one by one and put the syringe together.

"She has twenty units. She's not a bad case, just the one dose a day keeps her going."

"That's right," agreed the old lady sleepily, "just one dose a day, but, you know, I could give it to myself, Clara dear."

"That's right," Clara agreed, "so you shall in a couple of days' time."

Clara had just filled the syringe when the old lady spoke again.

"It's so curious, Judy dear, do you know, I thought just now I heard Mr. Jones come in and stand just inside the door, like he always did. It's as if he was saying, 'Come on, let's go for a walk, I'm waiting for you'."

Clara touched Judy's arm.

"You strip back the sheets and dab a little bit of spirit above her knee."

Judy did as she was asked, filled with relief that Mrs. Former was too sleepy to notice who was giving her the injection. Clara was clearly no novice; she slipped the needle in expertly and withdrew it and covered the old lady up and tucked her in.

"I'll just draw the curtains, I think, we don't want the morning light to disturb her." She pointed to the syringe now back on the tray. "Take that thing apart and put it back in the spirit, would you?"

Judy did as she was asked. Then she moved over to the bed. There was no sound at all from the old lady.

"She's asleep, I think," she whispered.

"That's right." To Judy's amazement Clara thrust her arm through hers. "We'll slip out, shall we?"

"Well," thought Judy, "I never thought I should be walking arm-in-arm with Clara. I suppose it's just a matter of stopping anywhere long enough and you become buddies, though, as a matter of fact, this buddyism, if Clara only knew, is a bit one-sided."

There was a large window half-way down the stairs, and out of it you could see the most beautiful part of the garden. Clara drew Judy to this window.

"There. That's something to look at, isn't it? Not over-looked, nice and remote, and our very own. Just a few repairs now and again. Plenty of money for that."

Judy was startled by Clara's voice. It had taken on an odd, gloating tone.

"Well, if you ask me, I think it's rather nice to have some neighbours and, as far as the money's concerned, I should think if the property were nearer the road the price would go up if Mrs. Former should ever want to sell it."

Clara continued to look out of the window. She was smiling.

"She won't want to do that. She certainly will never want to do that."

Judy always went to bed early, partly because there was nothing to do in the evenings, mostly because of her early start. She rather liked the time in bed before she fell asleep. She saw the rooks fly by the window cawing off to bed, and listened to the night breeze getting up, and let her mind travel till it reached The Bull Inn. Then she would shut her eyes and say to herself, "What's he doing now?" Sometimes she saw him playing a game of darts, sometimes smoking a pipe on the bench outside the inn while he talked to a couple of friends. Sometimes she knew he was out with the Home Guard. Sometimes she imagined him doing just what she was doing herself, lying on his bed with his hands behind his head, dreaming. She never got as far as to hope he was dreaming of her, she was quite sure he never did anything of the sort, in fact, it was practically certain that his dreams would be about his work. "What a queer world," thought Judy, "in which men spend their thinking time not on girls but on an explosive." To-night she knew that Nicholas was out with the Home Guard, and having mentally put him into his battle-dress she could go no further. What exactly Home Guards did on a night exercise was beyond her, but she still thought of him, and presently her eyes began to droop, she turned over on her side and prepared to go to sleep. She was just over the border between sleeping and waking when she heard a scream. In one second she was out of bed and into the passage. The screaming came from Mrs. Former's room. Judy had only taken a step towards it when Miss Rose almost fell out of the door, her face was greenish white and she was making animal moanings. She had, however, just sufficient strength left to realize that Judy was coming towards her. She tottered forward.

"Oh, Mother! Mother! I went in to kiss her good night. She was turning cold. She's dead, Judy. Dead." She fell in a heap on the floor.

CHAPTER IX

Judy did not go to bed again that night. She lay down fully dressed, and then, just before five, she got up, washed in cold water, did her hair and face and crept down the stairs.

"I don't suppose even a death in the house stops a woman like Clara from keeping to her routine," she thought. "Anyway, I'll be on the safe side."

The Bull looked as barred and shuttered as you would expect at that hour in the morning. Nicholas had one day shown Judy his window, and she had, of course, remembered which it was. Evidently Nicholas either did not read in bed or else pulled back the curtains before going to sleep. The black-out was not drawn, the window stood wide open. Judy went into the inn yard and picked up a handful of small stones, stood back well away from Nicholas' window and flung them in. In a moment Nicholas, with his hair on end, was looking out.

"Good Lord, woman! What's the matter? You hit me slap on the nose."

Judy peered up at him, longing for the actual feel of him.

"Oh, please come down. It's the old lady, Nick. She died last night. I'm terribly worried. I can't explain out here."

Nicholas was extraordinarily efficient In a very few minutes he was down the stairs dressed in a shirt and grey flannel trousers and had drawn Judy into the inn.

"I've put on the kettle," he said cheerfully, "and I've found the tea canister, so we'll soon have a cup of tea."

They sat on the kitchen table. The main rooms would not be very attractive, Nicholas explained, with the empty glasses and cigarette-butts lying around. Besides, in the kitchen they were handy when the kettle boiled.

"Now, come on," he said, closing one of his hands over Judy's, "out with it, let's hear everything from the beginning."

Judy started and got as far as the old lady's aversion to Clara's looking after her when shock, lack of sleep and misery got the better of her and she burst into tears.

"I'm so sorry," she wailed between sobs, "but I was fond of her, you know."

Nicholas pulled forward a chair and sat her in it. He knelt down by her, rubbing her hands.

"Poor little sweet, you shan't say one more word until you've had some tea, and no ordinary tea either. You're going to take Doctor Nicholas' prescription. I've just a drop of real honest to God French brandy upstairs, and it's going into your tea. That's what I believe in the best circles is called laced with brandy."

Warmed by the tea and strengthened by the brandy, Judy was able at last to tell her story. At the end of it Nicholas began pacing up and down the kitchen.

"Now, let's get things straight. The old lady had been put to bed by the doctor's orders."

"Yes. I wouldn't have believed Clara, but I've got Miss Rose's word for that. While I was away staying with you she tripped in the garden, and Clara sent for the doctor. The doctor told Miss Rose he thought the old lady was breaking up a bit and needed more attention, and was not to give herself her insulin."

Nicholas took two or three strides up and down the room in silence.

"What, of course, none of us know is what our dear Clara said to the doctor. What was the old lady's story of the tripping, did you get that?"

"She said there was nothing on earth the matter with her, that she did trip over a little bit of string, but she saved herself from a bad fall by coming down on her hands and knees, and was like that when Clara found her."

"Well, didn't Clara see she tripped over a bit of string?"

"No, she couldn't find it, and told Mrs. Former she'd had a giddy fit."

Nicholas lit two cigarettes and gave one to Judy. "Well, what happened then?"

"The old lady was put to bed, and Miss Rose was instructed to take away her hypodermic, but at this the old lady kicked up such a shindy that it was let pass for that night, but the next day, that was Monday, Miss Rose had to go scampering off to Doctor Mead who, to save trouble, came up and gave the injection himself, but at the same time told the old lady not to be naughty and to let herself be looked after for a day or two."

"So last night was the first night that either Mrs. Former herself or the doctor had not given her the injection?"

"That's right, but there wasn't a thing the matter with the injection, I saw that go in."

"Yes, so you told me. But don't let's go too fast. When you got home from work you went up and saw the old lady, and talked her into agreeing to let you give the injection."

"Yes, but I didn't actually mean to do it, you know. I meant to measure the dose for her and see she put it in properly herself."

"Now, tell me slowly about your conversation with Clara."

Judy went slowly over all that had been said.

"It's not very easy, as you can see. When she gets excited, words sort of fall out of her. Somehow she muddled it all up with Desmond, and there's not the faintest doubt that she's awfully proud of being a good nurse, and thought I was being rude when I said I was hospital trained."

Nicholas puffed at his cigarette, and it was quite a time before he spoke again.

"And in the end she agreed that you should help her give it. What caused that change of heart?"

Judy pulled her mind back to the kitchen and yester-day evening.

"Nothing at all. Desmond interrupted with his usual meaningless stuff and then, when Clara came back to her cooking, she was quite all right. She said she was sorry she had lost her temper, that to-night didn't matter very much because the old lady had been ordered some sedative and she's given it in some soup." Nicholas shot across the room and knelt in front of Judy.

"Sedative in soup! I wonder."

Judy shivered.

"You mean, you think she poisoned her?"

Nicholas thumped Judy's knee with his forefinger.

"Pull yourself together, my girl, you didn't come running to me in the early hours of the morning without reason. You came because you were frightened, and you were frightened because of the way the old lady died. It can't have been the insulin, you saw that put in and that the dose was right. Then what? If you were to nip back now, the bowl that soup was in wouldn't have been washed up, would it?"

Judy looked at him pityingly.

"People like Clara wash everything up right away. Particularly, I expect, if they've been using poison." Nicholas got up and held out a hand to her.

"I'll walk you home. You don't want to get Clara suspicious; it's quite natural that you should be upset and gone out for an early walk, but it's time you were back" Judy shivered. He looked at her. "You'll be all right all day, and I'll fix up somewhere for you to go tonight."

That was the kind of stimulant Judy needed. Up shot her chin.

"You won't, I'm sleeping in my own bed. If you think I'm going to leave poor old Miss Rose up there alone you're quite wrong."

Nicholas sighed.

"I knew you were going to say that. During the day I'll think up something so that it's easier for you to get hold of me. But what we've now got to think of is what is going to make Doctor Mead refuse to sign the death certificate without a post-mortem."

Judy glared at the road ahead of them.

"If Clara has really finished off the old pet you can bet anything you like that she's not left Doctor Mead to chance. I bet you anything that when he had that talk with her about the old lady's fall she laid all the trails."

"What did he say when he came last night?"

"Nothing that I know of. He was sweet to me, patted my hand and asked me to get some hot milk for myself and Miss Rose, and to give Miss Rose a sleeping-tablet. I don't know what he said to Clara, very little, I think. I heard him come out of the old lady's room, and then, as he locked the door, he said he'd be back in the morning."

Nicholas stood still.

"Locked the door?"

"That's right."

He let out a low whistle.

"It doesn't sound to me as though there's much grass growing on Doctor Mead. I don't think that you lock doors on what, I believe, the gravedigger described as 'people who died holily in their beds'. In other words, natural death. I seem to remember when my father died there was a great deal of coming and going. Great-aunts who wanted a look and to say a prayer, you know."

"Well, of course, it might just be that he hadn't been able to send up anyone to lay her out. Mightn't it?"

They were nearly at the private road. Nicholas stood still and took Judy by her shoulders and turned her to face him.

"It easily might, but I'm hopeful that it wasn't." He gave her a little shake. "Now, my little British lion, however brave you may be, look, on this occasion, like a wide-eyed innocent, and your Uncle Nick will be along to see you on your machine to hear the latest developments."

It was miserable in the house, and Judy was thankful when she had made some pretence at eating breakfast and was on her way to work. Miss Rose was still in bed sleeping, but Clara was downstairs, and, far from being depressed, had a kind of truculent gaiety about her.

"Such nonsense!" she told Judy as she put some bacon in front of her. "Doctor Mead is going to have a post-mortem. 'Why bother?' I said, 'I told you she was breaking up. Cut her up as much as you like, that's all you'll find'."

Judy shuddered and pushed away her bacon untasted. "She was such an old darling," she explained.

"Waste not, want not. It was easy enough for you to run round treating her like a prize poodle, but you didn't have to do for her. Anyway, she'd had her threescore years and ten. I don't believe in anyone stopping on after that. Give the younger ones a chance, that's what I say."

Judy found it extraordinarily hard to keep up her output that morning. She seemed to lack all energy, and it was with relief that she got a message in the middle of the morning that she was wanted in the office. In the office were the manager, a tall, good-looking man whom Judy up till then had only known by sight, and Doctor Mead. The manager drew up a chair for her.

"You know Doctor Mead, I understand, he wants a word with you." He turned to the doctor. "You can have this room as long as you like. I'll give orders not to have you disturbed."

Doctor Mead took out his cigarette-case and offered it to Judy.

"As I expect you heard this morning, I don't feel able to say of what Mrs. Former died, so I can't sign her death certificate, and that means a post-mortem, which is always an unpleasant affair. In this case it's a mere formality, probably the old lady was old and tired and wearing out, but it's my duty to be satisfied. What was your impression of her?"

Judy fixed the doctor with a direct glance.

"I thought she was wonderful for her age, and only really showed she was old in her deafness. I know she's supposed to have had a giddy fit and fallen over, but I think she's far more likely to have been right about the bit of string."

"Yes, that bit of string. I've not forgotten it. Now, tell me about this injection business. You saw it given, and you were partially trained in hospital, so you'd know how to give an injection."

Judy nodded.

"How big was the dose?"

"Twenty units."

"You saw it put into the syringe?"

"And into the leg. I cleaned the place."

Doctor Mead got up.

"It's extraordinarily unlikely that there's anything the matter, but, of course, we none of us can ever be too careful, can we?" He threw a sharp look at Judy. "Sleep last night?" She shook her head. "I thought not. I'll have a word with the first-aid post as I go out, and see if they've got somewhere you can lie down for an hour or two."

As Judy was coming down the office stairs to the works she found Nicholas waiting for her.

"I went to your machine. Shirley told me where you were. What happened?"

Judy explained.

"He never mentioned the soup or the sedative."

"Not a word?"

"No."

The offices ran round a gallery against the outer wall of the main workshop. Under the offices were various store-rooms. Nicholas opened the door of one and, finding it empty, drew Judy inside.

"Listen, darling. I'm not going to waste my breath on trying to get you out of that house. I realize that if you knew for certain that you were having a bowl of poisoned soup every day for a week you still wouldn't budge."

"Would you leave Miss Rose there alone?"

"I dare say I wouldn't, but as soon as we humanly can we must get her shifted, unless, of course, Clara is found to have put poison in the soup, in which case you and Miss Rose can live cosily together having fun and games with Desmond while Clara hangs by the neck until she's dead. In the meantime, however, I have a plan. Down that cobbled path at the side of the house and through that small gate, out where you took me to see the kennels and we found Mr. Jones, there's an outhouse, isn't there?"

"Yes. It's used for all sorts of things. Miss Rose makes butter and cream there on the sly whenever we have some extra milk, and Clara does washing there."

"Well, I propose to sleep there. There's a field path at the back of those kennels that I can get in by, and I'll take a couple of rugs and a portable mattress."

"But suppose you oversleep? What are you going to say if Clara finds you there in the morning?"

"She won't. All my life I've been able to wake up at any time I wanted. The only thing is, of course, the village will think I'm sleeping with you. Do you mind a bit of scandal?"

Judy flushed.

"Don't be such an idiot! But why are you doing it?"

He took her hand.

"Because I don't like Clara. I think she may be a murderess. Because there's no reason why you should sacrifice yourself to Miss Rose all on your own, and there's a third and rather useless reason. Because I'm very fond of a person called Judy."

Judy felt as if her heart missed a beat. She was suddenly conscious of the bench on which they were sitting, and the rows of sealed cans all round them, and the distant roar of machinery from beyond the closed door. "I'm very fond of you, Judy." What a darling little sentence and how beautifully he said it! She waited for more. When at last he broke the silence he was again back on plans.

"I shall be in that outhouse from ten every evening until five the next morning. At the present moment you'll have to come and fetch me if you want me, but I'll fix up something better than that before I'm through." He lifted her face in his two hands. "You'll be glad to have me, won't you?" Judy was hoping so desperately that he would kiss her that she found it quite hard to answer, but at last she managed a muffled "Yes, please". Then, to her disappointment, he got to his feet and took her by the hand. "Come along then. We've broken every law of decent behaviour in factories. One, no unauthorized person is allowed inside the stores. Two, though this one's unwritten, no man and girl employed by the firm must give an impression of wantonry carried on in the works. Good-bye, sweet, and don't forget when you tuck yourself into bed tonight to say, 'Good night, Nick, have a nice time with the mice in the outhouse'."

CHAPTER X

Nicholas stopped beside Judy's machine. He tapped her on the shoulder.

"They're expecting the result of the post-mortem this afternoon." Judy shuddered. "Really, for a sensible girl you're very silly about this post-mortem business. What difference can it make to the old lady, who, we hope, by now is sitting on a cloud having her first harping lesson, whether they cut up her frail old remains or not?"

Judy was used to hearing and being heard over the noise of the machines. She went on working while she talked.

"I don't believe for a moment that she's learning to harp. If heaven's at all like one hopes it is, she's found Mr. Former and they're looking after a lot of celestial dogs, including Mr. Jones."

"All right then, celestial kennels, but whatever it is it can't matter to her what they do with that old body she threw off down here any more than it matters to you what happens to the old coat you throw away."

Judy looked at him reproachfully.

"That's a very silly example. These days we women never throw away a coat. Certainly not in the happy-go-lucky way you describe. Are you coming to the concert?"

"Certainly I am. I even sent Mother a line to tell her that the works are going on the air and then she can sit by her wireless set, and say with a proud smile, There, that's my Nick's laugh, I'd recognize it anywhere!' Also, though you're so wrapped up in your house's concerns that I dare say it has escaped you, I'm accompanying our Shirley and hoping very much to get nicely announced for doing it. I think you might have guessed I should be appearing when you saw the advertisement 'Works Wonders'." He looked at her face. "Snap out of it, Judy dear. It's not doing you or anybody else any good to let it prey on your mind."

Judy tried to smile at him.

"Sorry. I do try, but it's the waiting gets you down. If you knew what it was like in our house! Miss Rose never stops crying and Clara keeps up a triumphant crowing about how stupid it is of Doctor Mead to hold a post-mortem, they'll find that the old lady died a natural death, and to add to it all, that little horror Desmond seems to like funerals, for he skips about the house singing, 'They're putting great-granny in a hole in the ground same as great-grandfather'."

"Well, it's your fault, there's no need for you to stay."

"What, and leave Miss Rose! Likely, isn't it? As a matter of fact her lawyer's been to see her. All things being equal she seems to be going to be quite well off. If we can find anywhere to go I think I could talk her into it and let Clara go on living in the house with Desmond."

"You're taking it rather for granted, aren't you, that the old lady died a natural death?"

Judy paused in her work for a moment and turned to him.

"I mustn't stop working now, but perhaps I shall get a chance to have a word with you in the canteen. I talked to Clara last night, and I must say, if she's apprehensive about the result of that post-mortem, then she's the most marvellous actress that ever lived."

The Works Wonders concert was going well. It was more formal than the usual canteen concert because, instead of the applause going to the more popular artists, it was regulated and conducted so as to cause a continuous roar of enthusiastic sound. Shirley was popular and her singing of "I'll walk beside you" was a natural riot. There were no encores so that when it was over Nicholas slipped round to the back of the room and sat on the piece of bench that Judy had kept for him. The works' band had just started on a medley of tunes, most of which were on the noisy side. They talked to each other in whispers.

"What did you talk to Clara about last night?"

"I didn't, she talked to me. She was feeding the chickens and I met her. It was about responsibility, really. She said that she thought we all had certain responsibilities for which we should be prepared to sacrifice everything. I thought at first that she was talking about the war, but afterwards, thinking it over, I wasn't sure. She was on a very highfalutin plane, believe me. All about caring for the weak and helpless who are in your charge. She said that was her faith and by that she lived. You must admit a person who feels like that wouldn't do in an old lady, would she?"

"Probably talking for effect."

"I don't think so. In any case you can find out for yourself because she said, amongst other things, wouldn't I like to bring you to the house, that you mustn't think that because we had a death we were morbid and wouldn't see visitors."

Nicholas grinned.

"Bit of a shock to her if she knew she'd got a visitor sleeping in every night, but I will come back with you after work to-day because they'll have got the result of the post-mortem, and I expect you'll find the house full to the brim of sleuths."

Judy turned a startled face to him.

"No! I thought they'd just send a Black Maria and take Clara away."

"Not at all, my poor innocent. Say the old lady has died of arsenic, everybody can be as certain as they like that Clara put it in her soup, but unless they can find that she had the arsenic in her possession they won't be able to do anything about her, and, as a matter of fact, if they find the old lady's died of poisoning, which I'm certain they will, I'm afraid poor old Miss Rose will be harried around a bit. After all, if she's going to be quite well off, it's she who gained by the death, not Clara." Judy gave him a pitying look.

"The woolliest-headed detective in the world couldn't suspect Miss Rose. Poor pet, she simply adored her mother."

"I know, my lamb, but the law's the law, and if somebody did the old lady in then they're bound to have a careful look over everybody who can have gained by it, that's why I'm coming back from work with you. I know how truculent you can be, and I don't want you to be truculent in defence of Miss Rose, it'll do more harm than good."

That evening Nicholas and Judy rushed out of the works and hurried up the road towards the old house. Nicholas offered Judy a drink to fortify her, but she was too anxious to waste any time. Ever since her talk with Nicholas in the canteen she had been haunted by a vision of silly, hymn-singing old Miss Rose being cross-examined by someone from Scotland Yard.

"I wish I'd known that there might be detectives up there," she said to Nicholas. "You know, Miss Rose is a pet, but she's an awful idiot, she won't know in the least what they're driving at, and, you see, she thinks she's got something to hide."

"What?"

"Milk off the ration to make butter and things like that. She's always thought that she is a big dealer in the Black Market. She's always kept it from her mother. Of course she is a silly old pet, it's just that when there's extra milk the house can have it, and the only person she has to keep it from is Clara, who wants everything extra for Desmond."

Nicholas took her arm.

"The Worry cow
Would have lived till now
If she hadn't lost her breath,
She worried her hay,
Wouldn't last all day
And she worried herself to death."

"A very good rhyme for you, my girl. Odd though it may seem, our detectives are excellent judges of human nature and won't be deceived by Miss Rose. They'll have found out all about her little hoards of food in two minutes, and got on to more important things."

As Nicholas and Judy came up the private road they walked in silence, their eyes strained at the gate in front of them. What would they see? Just outside the gate Nicholas paused.

"If we do find detectives here you've nothing whatsoever to be afraid of. Think carefully before you speak. Tell everything you know, and, above all, because some silly little thing may, in your opinion, look bad for Miss Rose, don't hold it back. The truth, exactly and all the time. It's the only thing when dealing with the law."

There was no sign of detectives. Instead a scene of remarkable calm met their eyes. Clara and Miss Rose were on the lawn sewing at some black material. In the distance

Desmond was playing some game of his own, hopping and skipping to catch something in the air. Clara looked up as Nicholas and Judy came towards her.

"How do you do? I'm glad you've come to the house, Mr. Parsons, it's been sad for Judy this last day or two." Judy could not bring herself to ask what she wanted to know, but she had to say something. She tried to pretend interest in their sewing.

"What are you making?"

Miss Rose tried to control her voice, but it wobbled.

"It's some black things of Mother's, dear. We're altering them to wear at the funeral. We haven't the coupons for anything new."

"And, in any case," said Clara briskly, "it would be a ridiculous expense."

"The funeral?" Nicholas spoke in a voice which neatly combined immense interest with suitable solemnity. "When is it?"

Miss Rose sniffed.

"The day after to-morrow. I am so glad they're letting her rest at last, poor dear. I didn't like all this cutting her up. They never did that with Father."

Nicholas sat on the ground at Clara's feet.

"No, very unpleasant. They've finished the post-mortem then?"

Clara let her work drop into her lap. There was a flush on her cheeks. She looked extraordinarily pleased with herself.

"They have, Mr. Parsons, and the result is exactly what I told them. Grandmother died a perfectly natural death, just Anno Domini."

Miss Rose had tears in her eyes.

"They couldn't find anything much the matter. Her heart just stopped."

Judy felt as if a cold hand had clutched hold of her. She turned her head to the side of the house where the little gate opened on to the path that led to the kennels. She heard again Nicholas' voice, "Just Anno Domini. He seemed to have nothing much the matter with him. His heart just stopped beating." She turned back to look at Nicholas. She could feel he wanted to say something. Clara's voice broke the silence.

"You'll stay for supper, won't you, Mr. Parsons?"

CHAPTER XI

WHILE Clara was getting the supper, Nicholas tried to get a word alone with Judy. It proved difficult. Miss Rose's wits, never of a very bright order, had become so slow since the shock of her mother's death that she was incapable of taking a hint. She sat squarely in her chair stitching, and kept up a continual flow of conversation, not, as Judy noticed pityingly, because she wanted to talk, but because she dreaded being alone with her thoughts.

"Mother bought this piece of stuff in London and had it made up in Bristol. Quite a tussle she had with Dad about it. Dad couldn't bear black, but Mother liked it; she said she had so little occasion to wear good clothes that people got to know them too well if they were coloured. One year, the King's Jubilee, Dad made her have a kind of purple with some cherry colour on it. She wore it, of course, on Jubilee Day for the processions and that, but she hardly ever put it on again. She said the moment it was on her she felt people were nudging each other and saying, 'Here's Mrs. Former in her Jubilee costume'."

Nicholas picked up a piece of the stuff which Miss Rose was stitching and felt it between his fingers.

"Very nice piece of stuff, isn't it? But I suppose she always bought the best."

"Oh, yes. Never wanted for a thing when Father was alive. Of course it wasn't always that way, the business had grown gradually, you know. Still, it was years since she'd wanted for anything, seemed quite queer, somehow, her thinking about money."

"I suppose your lawyers had to be strict. Death-duties are so heavy these days."

Miss Rose raised puzzled eyes.

"Oh, no. Mr. John's never said anything like that. He told Mother that we'd be able to live much the same as we always had. He told her there was quite a piece of capital she could use if she was short. Mother thought at first that would be all right, it was only when Clara explained to her that if she used capital other people coming after went without. Then, of course, she gave up all idea of spending it. I used to say to her, 'You use it, Mother, I wouldn't mind,' but somehow she'd got scared by then and left everything to Clara. Clara's wonderful with money."

"I expect your father was proud of her. A granddaughter with a business sense."

Judy was picking little pieces of grass and laying them in a small haystack in front of her. She looked at Nicholas out of the corner of her eyes, wondering if he was not going a bit far. Surely Miss Rose must grasp that she was being cross-examined, but she seemed blissfully unaware that anything but ordinary chat was going on.

"Oh, dear, no. He didn't believe in women knowing anything about business. My sister Millicent was Father's pet, you know, and Father wasn't really pleased when she married Arthur Roal. You see, he was a chemist and, Father thought, not good enough for Millicent. My poor sister Millicent died soon after her baby, Alfred, was born, and Father, though he tried to be just, always blamed Alfred a little, I think. I suppose he might have got fond of Alfred if he'd married just a simple, pretty girl, but instead, you see, he married Clara."

Nicholas' voice was deliberately casual.

"What did your father say when he first saw her?"

"He said, 'That damned chemist grandson of mine would marry a scrawny, black-haired thing like that,' and then he said," she lowered her voice, "for Father took a lot of interest in breeding, you know, it was his job, 'a woman with brains and that shaped head won't breed right, you'll see'." She cast an anxious look at the house to be sure her voice would not carry to the kitchen. "Then, you see, Desmond came."

Nicholas and Judy looked across the garden at Desmond. He was at some game of his own which necessitated his walking on all fours.

"Your father thought his prophecy right?"

Miss Rose leant towards Nicholas.

"Of course nobody ever admits it, but we have sometimes thought there was truth in it. Do you think he's a little different from other children?"

Nicholas slid past the subject of Desmond with a sympathetic grunt.

"Of course, when you're getting on in years you probably don't want your granddaughter and your great-grandson

living with you, especially if you aren't feeling too good."
Judy made a move to explain to him that Mr. Former
had died suddenly, but Nicholas stopped her with a quick
look. "When you're under the weather things tire you very
quickly, don't they?"

"Oh, but Father wasn't under the weather long," Miss
Rose protested. "He'd had mild influenza, you know, but
he went back to work. He seemed all right to myself and
Mother."

"Yes?" Nicholas queried.

"It was only when Clara pointed it out that we noticed
it. It was little things. He complained things were moved,
that the garage door was locked – just a lot of silly little
things, which, as Clara explained, were none of them true.
It just showed he was run down. She was very wise about
it. She said to Mother we mustn't let him suspect it was
she who first noticed he wasn't well, for it would have
annoyed Dad, and then he would have got into a tear. He
was as stubborn as a mule when he liked."

Nicholas looked up at Miss Rose with a smile.

"And what did your mother do?"

"She popped off to Doctor Mead and asked him to drop
in casually for a bite, just to see if he noticed anything
wrong. Mother told him, of course, why she was worried."

"And did Doctor Mead find something wrong?" Nicholas asked.

Miss Rose turned to Judy.

"You know how people were about Mother." Her voice
trembled. "Nobody liked to see her worried, did they, and
she had been in a proper state since Clara suggested that
Dad was ill. Doctor Mead said that he thought that he
might be better for a bit of a tonic."

Nicholas dug a little hole in the lawn with a stick.

"I bet that caused an uproar; not much of a tonic man, was he?"

Miss Rose smiled reminiscently.

"No. I can hear him now. 'When I need a tonic, Doctor, I'll give myself a good tablespoon of some stuff I give my bulls,' that's what he said. I forget now exactly how he got Father to agree to injections. I think it was just by promising him that he'd learn something out of it which he might find useful in his own job. Then Doctor Mead got him down to his surgery and gave him a thorough overhaul. I don't think he told Father that there was anything the matter with him, and he never told Mother. He told me and he told Clara. 'His heart's not too good,' he said, 'you want to keep an eye on him. Any sudden exertion might finish him off.' He told me not to worry, that he'd known hundreds of hearts like it that had lasted for years."

Nicholas was looking up at Miss Rose with an alert expression. He reminded Judy of a sporting dog on the scent of something.

"Then neither you nor Clara nor Doctor Mead were surprised at his dying suddenly like that?"

"Oh, yes, I was. You see, it wasn't as though he was in bed or anything like that. There he was walking about one minute and dead the next. I think the doctor was a bit surprised too. Dad didn't seem to have had a particularly tiring day, but then, as he said to me, we none of us knew what he might have been at, might have had a car breakdown and lifted something heavy. We never knew."

Clara came round from the side of the house and shouted, "Supper." Miss Rose laid down her sewing and got to her feet. Nicholas put a hand on Judy's arm and drew her back. He spoke in a whisper.

"See if you can manoeuvre Miss Rose off somewhere after supper. I want to have a word on my own with Clara."

It was rather a depressing meal, nor was there much to eat, so no one was sorry when Clara got to her feet.

"Well, I mustn't sit here any longer. I've got something to do if nobody else has."

Judy jumped at this opening.

"Nicholas, do take Mrs. Roal into the garden and give her a cigarette, she never stops working. Miss Rose and I'll wash up."

Clara opened her mouth to argue, but Nicholas took her firmly by the elbow.

"That's a good idea. Come on, Mrs. Roal, won't do you any harm to feel idle just for once in a way."

Clara did not want to sit in the garden, but she had no good reason for refusing. She gave in with a rather ungraceful shrug.

"Well, it won't hurt those two to do a bit of washing up, goodness knows. I won't be able to sit long, though. Desmond hasn't had his supper and I've got to put him to bed."

They were crossing the lawn. Desmond was not in sight, but they could hear shrill, tuneless singing. Nicholas nodded in the direction of the sound.

"Have a heart! Don't you remember what it was like to be in the garden on a summer's evening? With all the queer magic that there is on a summer's night, and to hear 'Come along now, time for bed'." He guided Clara to her chair and gave her a cigarette. "And then, upstairs in your nursery, looking out of the window at a world where everything seemed to be allowed to be awake except you."

Clara puffed at her cigarette.

"I was born in a town. I was the eldest of six, and I was thankful when I got a chance to get to bed. I had to lend a hand with the others first. We aren't all born with silver spoons in our mouths, you know."

"Judging by young Desmond's singing over there he isn't going to be glad to go to bed. You must be glad to be giving him so much better a time than you had yourself."

He had started a train of thought in Clara's mind. She spoke as if words were being pulled out of her.

"He's got to have a good time. I always swore he should. On the morning when they sent for me because our home and the business was gone it was Desmond I thought of. It was a fine business, always worth a nice bit if you wanted to sell the goodwill and all. The wardens wanted to stop me going in, there was a bit of the shop still standing, and they were afraid it might collapse, but I had to go in. It seemed as though, if I didn't force myself to see that everything was gone, I'd never believe it."

"Did you lose everything?"

"Yes. Some funny bits were saved, you know. Cakes of soap, cotton wool. Some of it I found lying about that first morning. I just had to pick things up, I . . ." she broke off. "Oh, here am I rambling along, don't know what made me talk about it, I never do."

"It's the shock of your husband's grandmother's death, I expect."

Clara gave Nicholas an almost laughing look.

"That was no shock. She'd had her threescore years and ten and then out, that's only fair. You don't want old people cluttering up the world, do you?"

"I don't know. Some old people I'm no end fond of. The little I saw of Mrs. Former I liked very much. Still, Judy tells me she'd never been herself since the dog died."

Clara got up.

"He was old, too. If there's one thing worse than an old human being it's an old dog. Smelly, greedy, nothing but sentiment keeping them about, if you ask me." She threw her cigarette on the lawn and ground it into the grass with her heel. "Good night, Mr. Parsons, I must go and give my boy his supper."

Nicholas left soon after that. Judy walked with him as far as the gate.

"Did you get anything out of Clara?"

"I don't know. I've got to think and perhaps it'll lead me somewhere. I'm going down to Doctor Mead now. I've had a bit of an idea. I'm going to get him to recommend a holiday for Miss Rose, then she can go to Mother and, meanwhile, you can come to The Bull."

"That'll cause a nice scandal. There won't be a soul in the works who doesn't know for a fact that I sleep with you every night."

Nicholas put an arm round her shoulders.

"Well, The Bull or somewhere. Now, hop along back and go to bed early, you look tired, and, besides, the sooner you all get to bed and lock the back door the sooner can Mr. Nick Parsons doss down in the outhouse." He turned to go and then came hack. "By the way, here's something for you." He felt in his inside pocket and brought out a whistle. "I've had this since I was a kid. It makes a particularly sharp and penetrating noise. I'd know it anywhere. Blow it like hell if you want me."

Judy took the whistle.

"Thank you, but I can't see why I'll ever blow it. Post-mortems can't be wrong, can they?"

"I don't know, Judy, my pet, it's one of the things I've got to think about. Good night."

Judy watched him out of sight, then she gave the whistle an affectionate little kiss. It was nice to think she owned something that belonged to Nicholas when he was a child. It was nice to think that it was there to blow if ever she should want to.

Doctor Mead was in his garden smoking a pipe and admiring his vegetables. He had treated Nicholas for one or two minor illnesses and got to like him. He nodded at him cheerfully.

"Hullo, young man! How are you?"

"Fine, thanks. It's not about myself that I've come this time. I've got a girl-friend at the works."

Doctor Mead tucked some stray pieces of tobacco into his pipe.

"Judy Rest. A doctor hears all the gossip, you know." He gave Nicholas a sharp glance. "What's wrong with the kid?"

"Nothing, but she's anxious about Miss Former. She wants you to recommend that Miss Former should go away for a change, and if you could do that I'd get my mother to have her."

Doctor Mead went on fidgeting with his pipe. His head was down, and Nicholas could not see the expression on his face, but he suspected it was more serious than the rather deliberately casual tone.

"And why is Judy Rest anxious about Miss Former?"

"She thinks she'd be better away for a bit."

Doctor Mead looked up and fixed his eyes on Nicholas.

"By that does she mean away from Clara Roal?"

"I should say that sums it up nicely."

"Well, you tell Judy Rest that the sooner that she and Miss Rose are out of that house, or the sooner that Miss Rose sends Clara and her boy packing, the better I'll be pleased."

"But you have rather a high opinion of Mrs. Roal, haven't you? It was you who put the old lady into her hands."

Doctor Mead laid a hand on Nicholas' arm.

"True, and it's not a thing I intend to discuss. But I admit now frankly to you, whom I know I can trust, that I've been very disturbed about that house. You know, of course, I went so far as to order a post-mortem."

"And she died a natural death."

"She was a diabetic, as you know, but the insulin was balancing that up all right."

"There was nothing else in unexpected quantities?"

"Nothing whatsoever. I didn't do the job myself. I was there and, believe me, I had a very careful look. If there'd been a thing wrong I'd have got an order to have the old man exhumed. He went just the same way, you know. Had a bit of a heart, but I'd hoped it would last him for years, but, mind you, his heart was in a sufficiently bad state for me to take it for granted that he died of heart failure."

"The dog went the same way. I had a private post-mortem on him."

"The devil you did! I wish you'd come to me then if you had any suspicions."

"The old boy died a natural death."

"In fact, you were in the same position that I am now. You didn't like it, but you hadn't got anything on earth to put your finger on. Two old people and a dog die of old age. There's nothing to link the three together. There's no point in any of it, no earthly reason why, if anyone is going to be suspected, we should suspect the Roal woman. On the face of it, it would be more likely to be Miss Rose, she'd something to gain."

"But do you suspect Clara?"

Doctor Mead shook his head.

"Suspect is too strong a word. There's just one little circumstance which links the death of the two old Formers. In both cases the story of their ill-health was brought to me by that woman."

Nicholas lit a cigarette and buried the match in a worm cast.

"But why should she want to do them in? They weren't all that much of a trouble."

"God knows. Matter of fact, between you and me, when I fixed up the post-mortem I had a bit of a look round for a motive, and I managed to run into the lawyer, John. Of course I didn't explain what I wanted to know, but I managed to find out something. No matter if every Former died Clara never benefits."

"What, not even after Miss Rose?"

"Not even after Desmond. There's a little sum in cash for the boy's education, and the rest goes into a trust which nobody can touch until he's eighteen. If the boy dies the whole lot goes to charities and so on."

"Then really, from Clara's point of view, it was better to have old Former alive and making money. He'd have kept them, I suppose. Time enough to push the family off the earth when Desmond was eighteen."

"Exactly."

Nicholas turned to go.

"All the same, you'd sleep a lot more comfortably in your bed if we could get Miss Rose miles away."

The doctor nodded.

"I certainly would."

"But otherwise you are letting the situation alone?"

Doctor Mead shrugged.

"What else can I do?"

Nicholas was turning to go, he paused a second. "Nothing, I suppose, as a doctor."

Doctor Mead lifted a questioning eyebrow.

"You mean what as a man?"

"Yes."

The doctor winked.

"I'll give any support or help I can to a younger man who has a more personal interest."

Nicholas smiled.

"Good. That's what I came to find out. Good night."

CHAPTER XII

NOBODY could possibly call the outhouse comfortable. Nor was life easy for Nicholas in sleeping there. Though he made his bed look slept in and was back in it before he was called he was quite certain that nobody at The Bull believed he slept there. Then there was the problem of the Home Guard, it was awkward for him after an evening exercise to slip away. It had been his custom, because he lived in The Bull, to have a last drink with the other men, and, though he was sure they would not meaningly spread gossip, it was hardly likely that the way he legged it every evening in the direction of the Old House would escape detection, especially as it was now light until close on midnight. It was a miracle really that no gossip had yet reached Clara. It was certain he must get Judy away and that meant getting Miss Rose away. It was all going to take a bit of manoeuvring. To-night, after his talk with Doctor Mead, he did not settle down to sleep as soon as he had laid out his mattress. Instead he took out a pencil and paper and began to write. He was disturbed by the creaking of the door and, looking up, he saw Judy. She was wearing a dressing-gown and pyjamas, and her hair, less sleek than usual, stood round her head like a halo. Nicholas eyed her sternly.

"Young ladies don't come into gentlemen's bedrooms in their night things. I am a sensitive man and I have got my reputation at the works to think about."

Judy sat down on the mattress beside him.

"Don't be an ass! And if you want to know, I've just as many things on now as I had in the daytime. I came to tell you that I don't think you'll be able to sneak up here much longer."

"Why? Has she heard something?"

"Yes. Our beloved little Desmond. It's extraordinary the way that child only seems to hear and see things that nobody wants him to hear or see. When he was going to bed to-night he called you the gentleman who came through the hedge. Fortunately, as far as I can make out, Clara just thought it was one of his crazy remarks. But he's a persistent child, he's sure to repeat himself. Great-grandfather going into a hole in the ground has become a kind of theme song. So might you."

Nicholas frowned at the paper in his hand.

"How could a child that goes to bed at about seven and gets up long after I've left possibly know that I sleep here?"

Judy hugged her knees.

"That's the queer thing about Desmond. I suppose because he doesn't use his senses like other people he gets more acute in other ways. I guess he saw the hole, and something of you left there; a piece of thread off your coat, or a button, or you might even have dropped a handkerchief, but Desmond read the sign just like gipsies do, and, without saying anything or even perhaps thinking it, he subconsciously registered that you arrived that way. Anyway, the little dear knows."

"Let him. I shall go on sleeping here until you and Miss Rose are out of the house, even if dear Clara has to know that I do it. I shall tell her it's love for you. A new form of gallantry."

Judy looked at the paper in his hand.

"Taken to doing your letters here? I must try and get you a desk. And maybe presently we can get water laid on."

Nicholas glanced down at the paper.

"Since you are here you might help me with this. It's a kind of examination paper, things I want to find out. One. What things are there in common between the deaths of the two Formers and Mr. Jones? Two. If there is anything in the world that could make people seem to have died of old age when they didn't. What is it and where could it be got hold of? Three. If Clara is never going to benefit by the will why should she want the Formers out of the way?"

Judy peered over his shoulder.

"Have you got any answers yet?"

"Doctor Mead gave me one about Mr. and Mrs. Former. He said the idea that either of them was ill came originally from Clara. Then, of course, there's another, they both died following the injections."

Judy shook her head.

"That's no good. I can stand up in any witness-box and swear to the insulin injection. There was nothing wrong with that nor with the way she gave it."

Nicholas frowned at the paper.

"All the same, I'm going to put those points down. Now we come to question two. You've worked in a hospital, can't you think of anything?"

"I shouldn't have thought there could be anything. You had poor Mr. Jones cut up to see what he died of, and Doctor Mead has had a post-mortem held on Mrs. Former, and everybody says it was old age in both cases."

"With reservations. The vet couldn't really say why Mr. Jones should have died, and Doctor Mead not only couldn't see why the old lady died but he was surprised about Mr. Former."

"But Mr. Former had a bad heart. Anybody might die of that."

"Yes, but when I spoke to Doctor Mead just now he said that though he had a bit of a heart he'd hoped it would last him for years. However, I'll leave that question and come to question three. Any views about that?"

Judy hugged her knees tighter and rested her chin on them.

"You say she gained nothing by the death of the two Formers."

"Nor would she by Miss Rose's."

"But does Desmond?"

"Yes, when he's eighteen."

"Then there could be an answer. I think Clara would be capable of doing anything for Desmond. She's kind of fierce about protecting him."

Nicholas shook his head.

"That's no good. During Miss Rose's lifetime there's only a money grant for Desmond's education. Anyhow he can't touch a penny until he's eighteen. Obviously, if old Former had lived, he'd have seen his only great-grandson decently educated, and both Clara and the boy would be living buckshee, so there was no possible point in bumping the old man off. If she was ever going to do it, somewhere near the time when he inherited the money would be the moment, and then bump off all three."

"Might be a bit obvious."

"Yes, but there would be sense in it and there's none now, and yet I'm as sure as I'm sitting here that there's been something very queer going on, and, though he wouldn't say so outright, Doctor Mead thinks that there was. I let him know I was going to snoop and he gave me his blessing."

Judy rubbed her fingers through her hair.

"Goodness, I do wish we didn't both feel suspicious. Here's the post-mortem over and the funeral will be over the day after to-morrow, and we might have settled down to some sort of domestic life, but here's us with our noses still to the trail."

He spoke gently.

"Yours needn't be. Nothing's likely to happen to Miss Rose just for a day or two. Why don't you move? After all, these people are nothing to do with you."

Judy peered at him through the growing darkness of the outhouse. But even in that light he could see the spark in her eye.

"I suppose I'm going to spend the whole of my acquaintance with you explaining that I'm not the sort of girl who backs out of things just because I don't happen to like them."

He rubbed her hair the wrong way.

"All right, my little lioness. The gentleman didn't mean any harm, don't bite him." His voice changed. "Seriously, Judy, I feel I've got to dig around in this business and I don't know where to start. Where do you advise me to begin? At question one, or question two, or question three?"

Judy was wishing that he would rub her hair again, but she kept any suggestion of that thought out of her voice.

"What connection is there between the deaths of the Formers and Mr. Jones? Then there's that one about what could have killed them, and then there's the motive. Have you got even a gleam of light on any one of them?"

Nicholas leant back against the wall.

"I feel one and two are really one question. I mean, if it was possible to find anything that looked like old age, then I suppose you could think of some connecting link between the deaths. There's just one possible idea, and, goodness knows, it's pretty vague. Clara's husband had a chemist's shop which was bombed. The morning after the bombing she went in and she picked up things that weren't ruined."

"Goodness! Aren't you the smart sleuth? However did you find that out?"

"She told me. She said that she only saved oddments, cakes of soap and cotton wool, but one never knows." Judy sighed.

"I should think it's a case of one never will. Even suppose she picked up a quart of prussic acid she's hardly likely to confide in you."

"No, but there are just a couple of outside chances on that. First of all to have a talk with the wardens, if possible with the ones in charge of that incident. They keep pretty good files, they might remember what was supposed to be in the shop, and, secondly, I thought you might search her room."

Judy's voice came out of the darkness with an amused note in it.

"Now, isn't that nice? I should just love to do that. Open all the drawers and the boxes and then get caught red-handed and be reported to the works as a thief."

"Well, it can wait. There's not much point in your doing it until you know what you're looking for."

"Oh, how I agree with you! There's quite a difference between looking for a quart of prussic acid or several containers of weed-killer."

Nicholas refused to be thrown off his trend of thought. "There's another thing you might do. You might make a bit of a friend of Mrs. White. I've always had a feeling that that woman hasn't said quite all she felt."

Judy got up.

"I suppose I ought to be going. I had a hell of a job getting down, the stairs creaked so, but, fortunately, Clara sleeps heavily, she gets up terribly early and I expect she's tired."

Nicholas got up too.

"I expect you're tired." He put a casual arm round her shoulder and sniffed at her. "You smell very nice."

For one second Judy had a thought of relaxing and leaning against him. What on earth would he say, she wondered, if she let herself go and put her arm round his neck and kissed him? Then the almost certain knowledge of what he would say pulled her together. She could hear his cool, collected voice, "Dear me! This is a very unexpected orgy, isn't it?" She gave him a little push.

"Go to bed. I'm like that flower stock that only smells at night. People come from miles around to smell me." She put her finger on the door and began gently easing it open. "Good night, Detective Inspector Parsons. I'll get down to being a buddy of Mrs. White's to-morrow."

CHAPTER XIII

ALL Pinlock, and such of the rural area around who could manage to get in, attended Mrs. Former's funeral. There had not been such local excitement since the war was declared. The Formers had been liked and respected locally, and Clara, with her managing ways, and her careful scrutiny of accounts and her attempt to get every bill reduced if only by a penny, was heartily disliked. The wildest rumours about her began to spread the moment it was known that the doctor had refused a death certificate. The chemist was supposed to have admitted selling her weed-killer. The vet, so the story ran, had sold her prussic acid to finish off Mr. Jones. The village woman, who came to Old House on Mondays to help with scrubbing and laundry, was supposed to have said that she had never dared touch a mouthful of food in that house, for she had always known what that Mrs. Roal was up to. It had been, therefore, a great disappointment to everybody when it was learnt that Doctor Mead had "found nothing", but so high was interest aroused by that time that few would accept such a mundane ending of their local scandal. People found excuses for attending the funeral. "I just had to make time, I was fond of old Mrs. Former."

"Of course I'll have to go, Mr. Former was a friend of my husband's. Poor man, he'd turn in his grave if he knew what was being said now."

"Poor thing, I just feel I must make the time to be at the grave, for only a fortnight back I read in my teacup there was danger for an old woman, and I said to my daughter, 'Mark my words, that's Mrs. Former.' I wondered then if I ought to go and warn her, and I never did and look what's come." Whatever their excuses and however truthful it was that they wanted to pay their respects to Mrs. Former, the large congregation at the funeral wanted to see how Clara was looking.

Any hope there was for a sensation was quenched as soon as the mourners arrived. It would have been impossible for anyone to look more correct, both in demeanour and clothes, than Clara. She had managed to turn Mrs. Former's old black into something suitable, but by no means excessive. Deep mourning or undue grief would have been entirely out of place in a granddaughter by marriage, and there was none. She stepped up the aisle most gently and considerately shepherding Miss Rose, and with the other hand keeping a firm hold on Desmond. Not one person present could think of a criticism to make. Only Judy, who, as an inmate in the house, had been given time off from the works to attend the funeral, and who had been considered a chief mourner, knew just how staged the whole entrance was. She had heard poor old Miss Rose the night before. "I want Judy to sit next to me in church. You will, won't you, Judy dear? It's what Mother would have wished." Clara had let that pass while Judy was about, but later that night Miss Rose, in floods of tears, had told Judy that it could not be. Clara had said that the front row of the church must be for family, that anything else would show disrespect. "There'll be lots coming to the funeral, Judy dear. Mother was much liked. Clara's right, I shouldn't like anybody to think we weren't showing proper respect." Judy longed to say, "Nonsense, don't believe the rubbish Clara talks," but she knew that she would only make things worse for Miss Rose. All she had said was, "Of course, I quite understand, and I shall sit in the row behind you, and you'll know I'm there if you should want me."

It was while they were standing round the grave that Judy saw Mrs. White. She was too full of thoughts of Mrs. Former at that moment to think of anything else. Miss Rose was dropping earth and tears on the coffin, and Judy was remembering the old lady pleading, "You won't leave us, Judy, will you?" She uttered a private prayer, "Oh, God, do let her have met Mr. Former and Mr. Jones, and let them be having a nice time together."

After the funeral Judy did not get into the mourners' car, for she had to get back to the factory. She was glad of the walk. The funeral had depressed her and she was thankful to be away from it. The late corn was being cut; there was a cheerful burr from the reapers and binders. As the wind touched the uncut com there was a flash of scarlet poppies. Scabious and harebells brushed against her ankles. Butterflies shot from flower to flower. There was life everywhere. It was wrong and foolish to go on sorrowing for an old lady who had lived her threescore years and ten and was perhaps glad to go. Her thoughts were disturbed by a pattering of feet behind her. Turning, she saw Mrs. White.

"My, talk about seven-league boots!" Mrs. White panted. "You don't half stride along. I thought you might wait for me, we're both going back to the works, I suppose."

Judy's mind shot away from Mrs. Former and came back to her promise to Nicholas. She had tried to find Mrs. White yesterday, but though she had seen her in the distance in the canteen she had not got near enough to have a talk, and now clearly this was her chance.

"How stupid of me! I might have thought of it, but my mind was miles away. I liked the old lady, you know, she was sweet to me."

"Ah! You've said a mouthful there. If it had been only the old lady and Miss Rose, believe me, I'd have been at Old House, Longbottom Lane, to-day. They were just the kind of people I like. Needed looking after, grateful for any kindness, and I'm one that likes looking after people, especially people of their sort, grateful for anything. You know, I don't mind telling you, I could have been knocked down with a feather when I heard that they'd cut the old girl open and found nothing."

"It didn't surprise me really. She had some soup the last thing with a sedative in it, and, of course, I couldn't swear what there might have been in that, but I did see the insulin injection given, and I knew that was all right." Judy paused a second thinking how to lead Mrs. White on to talk. She decided on frankness. "You know, everybody thinks there's something queer about the way the old Formers have died, but, as a matter of fact, Clara hasn't a thing to gain out of their dying. I mean, whoever else benefits, she doesn't."

"Who does then?"

"Miss Rose."

They were passing a gate. Mrs. White broke away from Judy and leant against the gate rocking with laughter.

"Oh, forgive me, dear, but a funeral's always taken me this way since I was a child. Go to a funeral and I act hysterical the same day. Oh, goodness! I don't half ache! Miss Rose, indeed! Miss Rose doing anyone in! I'd as soon suspect a new-born babe."

"All the same, she is the only person to gain, except that after her death everything comes to Desmond when he's eighteen. Why should Clara want Mrs. Former to die? You must admit it would be a silly thing for her to do to cut herself and Desmond off from their free board and bed, as it were. Mrs. Former didn't turn them out any more than Mr. Former did, but Miss Rose might. After all, Mr. Former had offered to make a home for his granddaughter by marriage and his great-grandson, and Mrs. Former was carrying on the same way. You must admit that Clara had everything to gain by their stopping alive."

Judy's words sobered Mrs. White. She took a packet of cigarettes out of her pocket, offered one to Judy and lit one for herself.

"Now, don't say a word for a minute or two, dear, you've set something going in my head and I can't think what." They walked along for quite a while in silence, then Mrs. White shook her head. "I can't get it. It was something that flashed into my mind from something you said, and now it's flashed out again. Can you think what you were saying and go back over it slowly?"

Judy tried to recall her words.

"I was saying that it would be silly for Clara to shut the door on hers and Desmond's free board and bread. Then I said that Mr. Former hadn't turned them out any more than Mrs. Former had done, but that Miss Rose might. That Mr. Former had offered to make a home for Clara and Desmond and . . ."

Mrs. White clutched her sleeve.

"That's it. That's what made me think. It was one Sunday not long before Mr. Former died. Mrs. Former and Miss Rose had gone to church and I was looking out of my window which, as you know, faces up to the gate. Mr. Former had gone out at the back to his kennels, and I suppose he found Clara there, for they began to talk. It was a still morning and I couldn't help hearing what they said. At first I didn't pay much attention and then afterwards I don't mind confessing I eavesdropped. I was downright interested and that's a fact! It was all to do with a Mr. Joseph Bloomfield. 'By the way, Clara,' Mr. Former said, 'I've heard from Mr. Joseph Bloomfield. He agrees with me it's the only thing to be done.' Then Clara said, 'Rubbish. It's far too early yet to be sure of anything'." Mrs. White gave Judy a nod. "That, of course, was when I started to listen. 'Well,' I thought, 'whatever's been going on'."

"What did Mr. Former say to that?"

"As far as I can remember he said, 'I'm sorry for you, my girl, but it won't do any good not to face facts. I've faced facts all my life and I can promise you that no harm ever came of it. Nothing but good, it's the only way to live'."

"And what did Clara say?"

"She said, 'I refuse to admit it's a fact, and you can't make me.' Then Mr. Former said – and that's why your saying that Mr. Former offered to make a home for Clara and Desmond put me in mind of the conversation – 'Oh, yes, Clara, my girl, I can make you. I'm still the piper, and the piper calls the tune. I know what's right and I mean to see it done, and you don't stop on in this house unless it's done, and, what's more, not one penny of my money goes where you know it's going unless you do things as I say.' They said no more, and a minute later Clara passed under the window. I popped back, not wanting her to see I'd been listening, but not before I'd seen her face. She wouldn't have noticed me though, and for once I was dead sorry for her. Her face was as white as a sheet and she was crying."

Judy chewed over this conversation in her mind. Who on earth was Mr. Joseph Bloomfield? What had Mr. Joseph Bloomfield agreed with Mr. Former was the only thing to be done? What on earth had Clara got to face? Whatever it was, she had to face it or be turned out and let Desmond lose his inheritance. Then there was a motive. One thing was certain, she must see Nicholas as quickly as possible, and she must somehow put Mrs. White off thinking that what she'd remembered was evidence against Clara. Mrs. White would talk, and talk just now might hinder Nicholas. She spoke in a deliberately amused voice.

"I know what that conversation sounds like, but I shouldn't think it was anything like that. Clara looks the soul of respectability to me. Anyway, it's certain that she did face facts, which I suppose included Mr. Joseph Bloomfield, because she went on living in the house and there was no row about her or Mrs. Former would have known."

Mrs. White dug Judy in the ribs.

"Say what you like, but there's something very queer about Clara Roal, and I'm not the only one who thinks that.

I don't want to see anybody had up for murder, but I must say if I had to pick and choose Clara'd be my first choice."

Nicholas and Judy left the factory together. They settled themselves under the tree where they had once picnicked with Mrs. Former and Miss Rose. Nicholas took out a piece of paper and a pencil.

"Now, have I got this right? In answer to your statement that Clara had a great deal to lose and nothing to gain by the deaths of the Formers, Mrs. White said that Mr. Former said that somebody called Mr. Joseph Bloomfield agreed with him that something or other was the only thing to be done, to which Clara replied with the rather curious statement that it was far too early to be sure of anything. A remark, one must admit, which sets the cleanest mind considering a delicate possibility. Then Mr. Former said that Clara ought to face facts, to which she replied that she refused to admit it was a fact, whereupon old Former said that as he paid the piper he called the tune, and that unless what he wanted to be done was done, she not only would not stop on in the house but not one penny of his money would go where she thought it was going. In fact, a proper scene out of a melodrama. 'Leave this house and never darken its doors again, and not one penny of mine will ever come your way'."

Judy leant against the tree-trunk.

"Allowing for a certain fertility of thinking on your part, that roughly was what she said."

"In other words, the motive. In a back to front way this answers my question three. I said, if Clara is never going to benefit by the will why should she want the Formers out of the way? The answer to that seems to be that she wanted Mr. Former out of the way because she believed he was going to force her to some course of action that she didn't want to take, and if she didn't do as he directed, he was going to alter his will, which would mean that her boy would never inherit. In fact, as pretty a motive as you could wish to find, but all hanging on the uncorroborated evidence of Mrs. White."

Judy leant forward and studied the paper in Nicholas' hand.

"I suppose Mr. Joseph Bloomfield would corroborate if one could find him."

Nicholas offered Judy a cigarette.

"A woman is usually much cleverer about women than a man. Would you say it was possible to read into that conversation Mrs. White overheard that Clara was going to have a baby?"

Judy shook her head.

"Most unlikely. To begin with, who was the father? And, from another point of view, if there was a man in her life, why, if she got rid of Mr. Former, should he disappear? I mean, quite obviously if it was that sort of reason, once Mr. Former was out of the way Clara could have gone on with her love-affair. There is also the question – where's the baby?"

"Well, Clara may have been right when she said it was far too early to be sure of anything."

Judy flicked some cigarette ash off the end of her cigarette.

"I don't believe it's possible. None of it sounds like Clara."

"I know," Nicholas agreed, "but, on the other hand, it's the most obvious motive in the world. If you were to look through the histories of women murderesses I'd take a bet that the majority did their victims in because of a love-affair, and often the victim was the person who discovered the love-affair. What you might call a respectability murder."

"Well, if you're right, Mr. Joseph Bloomfield is a gynaecologist and he runs some sort of home in which babies are born, and in that case what Mr. Former said was that Mr. Joseph Bloomfield was certain that Clara was going to have a baby, and since they didn't want a local scandal, the only answer was that she should go away, presumably to Mr. Bloomfield's home."

Nicholas got to his feet and held out a hand.

"Come along, sweet. You've hit the nail on the head. Mr. Joseph Bloomfield is a gynaecologist, in which case he's in the medical register and our Doctor Mead will have a medical register."

Judy looked at her watch.

"It's sickening but I can't come with you. It's my suppertime and I mustn't be late. You go on your own and I'll pay another evening visit to you to hear the answer."

Nicholas looked annoyed.

"Blast that house! Even if it wasn't kept by a possible murderess it's sickening the way you've always got to be in for something or other. Why not come and have supper with me at The Bull?"

Judy was enormously tempted, but she resisted it.

"I'd love it. Oh, goodness, I'd love it! Supper away from Clara. But I can't. Poor old Miss Rose will be in the depths to-night after her mother's funeral."

Nicholas put an arm round her.

"I dislike being personal, but I must admit you really are the nicest girl I ever knew. See you to-night."

It was nearly midnight when Judy slipped into the outhouse. Nicholas grabbed her arm.

"I thought you were never coming."

Judy spoke in a whisper.

"It's been a risk. I believe Clara has been investigating Desmond's story about the way you arrive. Anyway, I'm certain she's suspicious of something, so I simply had to wait until I was certain she must be asleep. And, incidentally, will you please notice after your rudeness the other night that I'm fully dressed in slacks and a shirt, or rather you can't see that I am, but I'll tell you so that you don't come all over Victorian and anxious. Did you find Mr. Bloomfield?"

"No. The wretched fellow is not a doctor. I had to wait half an hour for Doctor Mead; he's got a medical directory all right, but we couldn't find him anywhere. There's just one queer thing, Doctor Mead knew his name. He said he was perfectly certain that he'd heard it somewhere. He thinks it'll come back to him and then he'll let me know."

Judy laid a hand on his arm.

"Do you hear anything?"

Nicholas grew tense.

"Yes. Get in the corner." He stood beside her with an arm round her. He put his lips to her ear. His voice was hardly a breath. "If she's got a torch and looks in she'll see my mattress. Do you think she's been to your room?"

Judy pulled his ear to her mouth.

"I've left a lump in the bed that might be me. Sssh!" They clung together, their ears straining. If Clara was outside she was moving with extreme caution. There were faint sounds which might be footsteps, and then nothing. Suddenly there was a creak and the door began to open.

It remained open for what seemed to Judy and Nicholas an eternity. Then it was closed again. They still said nothing, but waited until once more they heard the sound of the back door.

Nicholas mopped his forehead.

"My word! That was a near thing! It was a miracle she hadn't got a torch. I thought every second I was going to sneeze."

"I'd almost be thankful if she had caught us. I may tell you I think absolutely nothing of going back into that house. I'll get the horrors feeling she's going to pop out somewhere."

"What do you suppose she wanted?"

"To catch the two of us together, I should think. The most perfect way of getting rid of me, which we know she wants to do. She's only got to report to Mrs. Edwards that I'm no better than I should be and I'll be out of the house in three minutes."

Nicholas still had his arm round her.

"Is there a ladder on the place?"

"Yes. Down by the apple trees."

"Then, my love, in due course I shall fetch it. You can't go back through that creaking back door. You'll have to get in by your window."

Judy giggled.

"What a story it sounds! What a bad character she could make me out if she saw me come in."

Nicholas, in the darkness, found her chin and turned her face to his.

"Seems a pity that you should be accused of goings-on for nothing. Would a kiss come amiss?"

CHAPTER XIV

JUDY climbed over the sill and towards her bed. It had been lovely in the outhouse with Nicholas, but, since she had to get back sometime, she was glad to have achieved the journey. She had heard a faint scrape as Nicholas, having waited to be sure she was safely in, removed the ladder. He seemed to have feet like a cat, for even with the weight of the ladder in his arms, strain her ears though she would, she heard no sound of his footsteps. She stood by her bed and slipped off her slacks and shirt, and was just stretching out for her nightdress when she froze. There was someone else in the room.

Judy remained for a few seconds exactly as she was, one arm stretched out for her nightdress. In the first second her heart seemed to somersault, then she forced down panic and made herself think. Who was in the room? Almost certainly Clara. What was she in the room for? Judy's first reaction to that question was fear, then common sense pushed terror aside. Clara was here to spy. Standing perfectly still in the darkness Judy strained to hear where she was standing. The slight sound which had made her conscious she was not alone had come from the door end of the room.

Judy had not put up with the one naked electric light hanging from the middle of her ceding, she had sent home for a bed-side lamp and a length of flex. What she would like to have done at that minute was to flick on the lamp and face Clara, but the lamp was the far side of the bed, and to walk round that large double bed with Clara standing motionless by the door was more than she could face, but by the bed-side lamp there lay something that she wanted now more than she wanted light. Nicholas' whistle. If only she had that in her hand she felt she could tackle Clara no matter for what reason she was in her room.

The decision as to what to do was taken out of Judy's hands. The long pause was evidently a strain on Clara. She moved, and in moving touched the little washstand by the door, which caused the jug to rattle in the ewer. On a windless night in a house which had neither cat nor dog jugs could not rattle in ewers without causing comment. Judy sprang on to the bed and, as she leant across to her light switch, called out, "Who's there?"

Clara stood composedly between the washstand and the door. She had on a tailored-looking green dressing-gown, against which her skin looked exceptionally white and her eyes and hair unusually dark. Judy decided that polite amazement was the only tone to take.

"Good heavens, Clara! How you startled me! Is anything the matter?"

Clara looked at Judy, who had covered herself with the sheet.

"I think it's you who should answer that. It isn't I who have come in through the window, undressed, in the middle of the night."

Judy had found the whistle and felt as brave as a lion.

"Undressed nothing, I was wearing a shirt and slacks. Have a look, there they are."

Clara did not bother to look at Judy's slacks on the chair. She went straight on as if Judy had not spoken.

"You realize that you will have to leave in the morning."

"I understand nothing of the sort. It may be rather unusual to pop in and out of windows in the dead of night, and I don't mind confiding in you, since we're all girls together, that I went to meet Nicholas, but I can assure you we behaved beautifully."

Clara obviously did not care in the least what Judy had been up to. To get rid of her was the only thing in which she was interested.

"I tell you you'll leave to-morrow. I shall go and see Mrs. Edwards myself first thing."

Judy stretched out her hand for her nightdress and put it over her head.

"You've forgotten something, haven't you, Clara? It's not for you to say whether I go or not. It rests with Miss Rose."

The mention of Miss Rose stirred something in Clara. She flushed and came to the foot of the bed. Her words fell over each other.

"You think that you can influence Aunt Rose, don't you? Everybody thinks that they're going to interfere with Aunt Rose. There's Doctor Mead saying she's to have a holiday, there're all kinds of people peeping and prying. 'What are you going to do now, Miss Former?' 'Shall you live on in this house, Miss Former?' Now I'll tell you something. Aunt Rose is going to live on in this house, and Aunt Rose is not going to have a holiday. I've made my plans for Aunt Rose and she's going to be perfectly happy with me. You know how she hates a row. Well, if you force it there's going to be a row tomorrow morning. If you make Aunt Rose decide whether you go or stay you'll be sorry. You just go quietly and leave Aunt Rose to me."

With the whistle gripped firmly in her hand Judy felt a match for ten angry Clara's.

"My dear woman, don't take that bullying tone with me. I've done nothing whatsoever to be ashamed of, and if it interests you I'm perfectly prepared to go to Mrs. Edwards tomorrow and tell her all about it. In the meantime, listen to this. Unless Miss Rose asks me to leave this billet, here I stop, and all your prying and snooping and arguing won't make any difference. Now for goodness' sake go to bed. I want some sleep if you don't."

For one moment it looked as if Clara were going to do something violent. She pulled herself taut and stood poised, then she relaxed. She walked to the door. Before she opened it, she turned.

"You say you like Aunt Rose. If that's true you're doing her anything but a kindness in this attitude you're taking. If you want to help her, you find a new billet to-morrow."

Judy waited till she heard Clara's door shut. Then she got off the bed. She went to the window and rearranged the black-out. She looked at the lock on her door, then opened the door softly. She made a face. There was no key. She wandered round the room considering the furniture. There was the large mahogany wardrobe, it would take two strong men to move that, as it would the double bed. She went to the corner and leant against the mahogany chest of drawers. Of course she could not move that to-night, but perhaps she could in the morning. If it were at the other end of the room she could at a pinch shove it against the door. One moment's pushing showed her the futility of this idea. The chest of drawers weighed as much as the other furniture, there was no hope that she could move it.

Judy got back into bed and considered the situation. Even supposing that Clara had murdered old Mr. Former and Mrs. Former and Mr. Jones, there could be absolutely no reason for her murdering Miss Rose. Miss Rose owned this house and paid the bills, and if she were going to die, all that Clara would get would be a lump sum down and

Desmond an income when he was eighteen. It could not make sense. Whatever else Clara meant to do, it could not be that. Yet she did want her out of the house, she always had. Why? It was most unlucky that she had been discovered getting in at the window, that did give Clara a case of a sort. But the decision as to whether she was to be turned out rested with Miss Rose, and Miss Rose was incapable of thinking evil of anybody. She might think it a little dashing prowling up and down ladders to meet Nicholas, but she certainly would not think there was any harm in it. Yet there was no doubt at all that Clara would fight to get her out of the house, she had said it would not be kind to Miss Rose to let that fight take place. What, in the name of wonder, did it all mean? She would see Nicholas in the morning and tell him what had happened. But could she? What was he going to say when he heard that Clara had been in her room and she had no means of locking her out, or even of putting a piece of furniture against the door? He would go to everybody and make a row. Up till now, though he had hated her being in the house, the thought of personal danger to her had never crossed his mind, yet if she stayed on against Clara's wishes there did seem a faint danger. People said if you poisoned one person you made a habit of it. Suppose Nicholas was right and Clara had got hold of something which didn't show at the post-mortem. Judy found she was clutching the sheets and her hands and forehead were sticky. She gave herself a mental shake. "Oh, for goodness' sake pull yourself together and don't be morbid. It's only for a day or two anyhow. Miss Rose is going to be got away for a holiday whatever Clara thinks, and then you can leave. In the meantime, when Nick says, as he will, 'Why didn't you lock your door?' for peace and a quiet life say, 'Because I was an ass and I will next time'." She lay down and turned out the light. In the hand tucked under her chin she clasped the whistle. "Now breathe deeply and think of something nice," she ordered herself. As she took her own advice she felt the strain and fear of the last half-hour slipping out of the room and in its stead Nicholas' arm round her, and his lips against hers, and heard his voice whisper, "Would a kiss come amiss?"

Clara was a most unpredictable person. It was difficult for Judy to know exactly what she had expected the next morning, but whatever it was she certainly did not expect nothing to happen at all. Clara called her as though they had not met a few hours before. Breakfast passed off with no reference to Judy's leaving, and though Clara walked with her as far as the door, she said nothing more about visiting Mrs. Edwards. All the same, Judy thought as she hurried down the private road and out of the gate, she's up to something, but what?

Judy got her answer at three o'clock that afternoon. Mrs. Edwards stood beside her.

"Will you come along to my office for a moment, dear?"

Mrs. Edwards' office was at the end of one of the galleries which ran round the works. It was quite a distance away and, as Judy followed her through the factory and up the stairs, she considered her plan of action. By the time she was facing Mrs. Edwards across a desk she felt serene. She leant forward, resting on her elbows and gazing straight into Mrs. Edwards' face.

"Clara Roal has been to see you to ask you to move me somewhere else because of my goings-on at night."

Mrs. Edwards looked worried.

"Is it true?"

"It's true that I climbed in at my window last night. It's true that I was meeting a man, Nick Parsons to be exact, but it's not true that there were any goings-on."

"None at all?"

Judy flushed.

"I'm not going to lie to you, he kissed me, just once."

Mrs. Edwards glanced down at some notes in front of her.

"You left the house just before midnight and you didn't come back until nearly two." She laid down her notes. "Come on, what is all this about, what are you up to?"

Judy countered that by another question.

"Have you heard anything about that house I'm in?"

Mrs. Edwards smiled.

"My dear girl, if one was deaf and blind I don't think one could live in this place in the last couple of weeks and not have heard of your house."

Judy fiddled with a pencil on the desk.

"I know you're a welfare supervisor and you've got your job to do, but do you think, just for once, you could let something slide? I mean, could you possibly tell Clara Roal that you'd seen me and that I'd admitted my crime and you were getting me a new billet, and then do nothing about it for a little? I wouldn't ask this for nothing, honestly, and this I swear, I was doing nothing wrong last night."

Mrs. Edwards was silent for a moment or two.

"Last time you saw me about this billet, you told me it wasn't Mrs. Roal's house and she'd no right to query whether you stayed or didn't, it was up to Mrs. Former to decide. Now I understand that the decision rests with Miss Former. It is she who wishes you to go."

Judy gaped.

"Clara told you that? It's the most awful lie. Poor old sweet! Miss Rose would never believe harm of anybody. If Miss Rose caught me out behaving worse than anyone else has behaved before or since, she'd be certain that her eyes had deceived her."

"All the same, unless I've proof to the contrary the message has come from Miss Former. How does that affect the situation?"

Judy hesitated.

"I'm in a bit of a hole. I don't really want to have to tell you any more, but I swear to you that I'm doing what I think right, and that I shan't want to stop on in that house very long because we're going to get Miss Rose away for a holiday, and the day she leaves, the old house won't see me for dust anyhow, so if you could possibly look as though you were doing something, and were really doing nothing, it would be a marvellous help."

Mrs. Edwards took a sheet of notepaper and picked up her fountain-pen. "If I'm sending a note up to the house should I send it to Miss Former or to Mrs. Roal?"

"If it's to say you're finding me a new billet as soon as possible you might send it to Clara, it'll make for peace and a quiet life. I'm certain she was lying when she said Miss Rose wants me to go. Miss Rose and I are buddies, but it won't help the situation just now to find Clara out in a lie."

Mrs. Edwards wrote, read through what she had written, blotted it and passed it to Judy.

"How's that?"

The note said: "Dear Mrs. Roal, I am sending you this note by Judy Rest herself; she does not deny your statement. I've told her that Miss Former wished her to move, and that I expect to give her the address of her new billet in the course of a day or two. Yours sincerely, Lola Edwards."

Judy passed the letter back.

"Quite perfect. You might have been dealing with people like Clara all your life."

Mrs. Edwards put the letter into an envelope and addressed it and held it out to Judy.

"I'm trusting you, but not, you understand, indefinitely. I think it's a good idea you should leave that house. You say you're getting Miss Former away. What arrangements have you made?"

"Nicholas Parsons is getting his mother to invite her to stay."

"When?"

Judy took the envelope and got up.

"I'll get the whole thing put in order this evening." Mrs. Edwards shook her head at her.

"You're a very masterful young woman, but I'm not at all sure I'm doing the right thing. I'm not in the least worried about your behaviour, but I am a little about your being in that house. You swear to leave the moment Miss Former gets away?"

Judy laughed.

"I shall move into The Bull and then you really will have to worry about my morals."

Mrs. Edwards was not in a laughing mood.

"You'll take steps about getting Miss Former away tonight?"

"Yes."

"Very well. I'll give you a week. At the end of a week, whether Miss Former's gone on a holiday or not, I shall put you into a new billet."

Nicholas walked home from work with Judy and heard everything that had happened.

"One week," he said. "Well, there's nothing for it but Mother will have to come here in the flesh and take Miss Former back with her. I shan't sleep in the outhouse to-night, I'm going to rove, and most of my roving will be under your window. You've got your whistle?"

Judy produced the whistle which was hanging round her neck.

"After last night I won't be parted from it night or day."

"And after last night you'll sleep with your door locked. Is it a reasonably good lock?"

Judy had been prepared for the question, but she hated lying to him.

"Perfectly all right."

"I'm going to see Doctor Mead again to-night in case Mr. Joseph Bloomfield has come back to him. Would you like to come to London with me on Saturday afternoon? Have you anywhere you could stay?"

"I've got a cousin who lives in an hotel in Kensington. I could wire her to get me a room. What are we going up for?"

"I've been on to a friend who's a big bug in London's Civil Defence Service, and asked him to see what he can do to dig out the incident officer and anybody else who dealt with the incident on the Roals' chemist shop. He says he'll do what he can and he'll have them on call on Sunday morning."

They were nearly as far as the Old House private road. Judy loitered.

"I should adore it, but I don't awfully like leaving Miss Rose alone for the night."

"I don't honestly think you need worry about her, except from a loneliness point of view. I've been backwards and forwards and sideways over the situation and I simply cannot see what Clara would have to gain by getting rid of her."

"She'd nothing to gain, if it came to that, in getting rid of Mrs. Former or of Mr. Jones."

Nicholas opened the gate for Judy.

"Do you suppose anyone would murder somebody to save themselves trouble? I mean, there was point in Mr. Former dying, with Mrs. Former dying and Mr. Jones there's trouble saved, and as far as board and lodging are concerned she's not a penny the worse."

"As long as Miss Rose keeps on Old House, you mean?"

"That's it." He patted Judy's shoulder. "Pop along to supper, sweet. Don't worry if you don't hear me, the moment it's dusk the little sleuth will be under the window."

Judy was still thinking of what he had said about Miss Rose.

"What are you going to do about your mother?"

"Phone her to-night. I'll get a room for her at The Bull."

Judy walked thoughtfully through the gate.

"If you were by any chance right, the less anyone knew about Miss Rose going away the better, don't you think?"

"Infinitely better. I shouldn't wonder if we nipped her off at a second's notice without her luggage."

Judy was feeling low-spirited, but she did not want Nicholas to know it. She waved good-bye and gave him a particularly radiant smile.

"You really are marvellous. I don't know what we poor girls would do if there weren't you men with your wonderful brains to look after us."

CHAPTER XV

Old House had, since Mrs. Former's death, become just a roof to Judy. She never from choice went inside the drawing-room. The old lady's armchair was still in the window, and though Clara had tidied the room, no tidying could sweep away that frail ghost. It seemed to Judy that she must hear the old lady's voice saying, "Here you are, dear," and that she herself would answer in the raised voice which could reach deaf ears, "How have you been behaving to-day?" To-night she walked into the house on tiptoe, hoping that no one would hear her arrive. Clara must have her note as soon as possible and she must be given it when Miss Rose was not about.

Clara, Miss Rose and Desmond were in the kitchen. Judy turned towards the stairs, meaning to tidy up first and catch Clara alone later on, but at the bottom of the stairs a scrap of conversation coming from the kitchen stopped her. Clara was speaking apparently to Desmond.

"Don't pick that up yourself, Desmond, let your great-aunt do it. If she doesn't do it quick enough, give her a kick."

There seemed to be no answer from Miss Rose to this. Presently Desmond spoke in his usual inconsequent manner.

"I kicked a sheep once."

Clara answered him slowly and carefully, obviously intending her words to sink in.

"That's a clever boy, and the sheep made a baa and it ran, didn't it? But your great-aunt won't baa and run, you kick hard and try. Go on, do as Mother says."

There was silence and then a little grunting moan. Judy felt quite sick. What on earth could Clara be up to? Had she gone mad? Poor darling old Miss Rose! In a fury Judy stalked along the passage and flung open the kitchen door.

Miss Rose was on her knees scrubbing the floor. Clara was leaning on the kitchen table looking at her. As Judy came in Desmond, making baaing noises, ran forward and gave Miss Rose what was clearly one of a series of kicks. Judy forgot about tact and keeping on good terms with Clara. She seized Desmond by the arm and shook him till the child's teeth rattled in his head.

"Don't you dare do that, you loathsome little horror!" Clara shot round the table and pulled Desmond away from Judy.

"Leave him alone. How dare you touch him!"

Judy, stammering with rage, faced Clara.

"I like that! How dare he kick Miss Rose?" She knelt down beside Miss Rose and put an arm round her. "It's a shame, but you shouldn't be such a meek mouse. Why didn't you kick back again? I would." Miss Rose did not seem to hear what Judy was saying, but went on scrubbing the floor. Judy gave her a shake. "Listen to me, Miss Rose darling, you should stand up for yourself in your own house." Still there was no response from Miss Rose. Judy gave her another gentle shake. "Do stop scrubbing and listen to me." She looked up at Clara.

"She shouldn't do this heavy work after all she's been through. Never mind, Miss Rose darling, you're going to have a holiday, aren't you?"

Clara led Desmond to the back door and pushed him outside, then she turned to Miss Rose.

"I think you want to say something to Judy, don't you?" There was no word from Miss Rose. Clara raised her voice. "You want to say something to Judy, don't you?"

Miss Rose clambered awkwardly to her feet. She looked at the floor while she was speaking.

"I don't want a holiday. I want to stop here."

Clara nodded approvingly.

"And why do you want to stop here?"

Miss Rose still eyed the floor, fidgeting with her scrubbing apron. She stammered a little, looking at Clara anxiously out of the corner of her eyes.

"I want to stop here to be with Clara and dear Desmond."

"Go on," Clara ordered, "there's more than that."

Miss Rose looked nervous. There was a question in her voice, as if she were making sure she was getting her statement right.

"And I don't want a holiday."

"Go on," said Clara. "What about Judy?"

Miss Rose flushed and there was quite a pause before she spoke again.

"And I don't want Judy to go on living in my house. I'd rather she found a billet somewhere else."

Judy was so stunned at the whole scene that for a second she did not quite know what to do. Then common sense came to her rescue. Whatever all this did or did not mean, it was certainly not Miss Rose's fault. She went up to her and put an arm round her.

"Look at me."

There was a pause.

"Look at her," said Clara.

Another pause and then Miss Rose raised her eyes. Judy gave an exclamation and tightened the grip of her arm.

"Miss Rose, sweet, what on earth's the matter? You look scared to death. There's nothing to be scared of. It's a free world, you're living in your own house, nobody can make you say or do anything you don't want to do."

For one second it looked as if Miss Rose were going to be her natural self and break down and cry, or at least hug Judy and tell her what was wrong. Then Clara broke in again.

"Go on, Aunt Rose. You don't want Judy to think you're being bullied, do you?" Her voice changed, there was a meaning behind it which Judy could not place. "It would be very unfortunate for you if Judy thought that."

Miss Rose visibly pulled herself together. She jerked herself out of Judy's arm.

"Nobody is making me do anything I don't wish to do."

"And all you want," Clara prompted, "is to be left alone to manage your own affairs and Judy to leave the house as soon as possible. That's right, isn't it?"

Miss Rose kept her face turned from Judy.

"That's right."

Judy went up to her room. She opened the window wide and leant on the sill and gazed out at the gate. It was nice to look at the gate, for through it lay freedom from this queer, unwholesome house, and through it lay Nicholas. This, however, was no time to think of Nicholas or how nice it would be to live somewhere else, this was the time for clear thinking. Nicholas was wiring for his mother, but what good could Lady Parsons do with Miss Rose saying it was her wish that she should not go away? Why was Miss Rose behaving like this? What, in heaven's name, had Clara got hold of to scare the old girl, for that Miss Rose was too scared to do anything but what she was told was certain. Accepting the fact that Miss Rose was scared of something, what was Clara going to get out of it? Fond she might be of Desmond, but nobody but a lunatic could wish to show their fondness for their child by teaching it to kick its elderly relatives. Then the sentence she had heard at the bottom of the stairs came back to her: "Don't pick that up yourself, Desmond, let your great-aunt do it. If she doesn't do it quick enough, give her a kick."

"Don't pick that up yourself, Desmond, let your great-aunt do it." It was all very frightening. It simply did not make sense. It sounded like the worst sort of story you heard about the Gestapo. What should she do now? She could walk out of the house and find Nicholas and ask his advice, or she could go on as if nothing had happened. Obviously the walking out of the house and finding Nicholas would be the pleasantest thing to do, but what about the right thing to do? If she walked out and stayed out to supper it was the first step towards giving in to Clara. Miss Rose was a gullible, dear old silly, she was scared stiff, no one but a cad and a coward would give in one inch. Sighing, Judy turned from the window and began tidying her hair.

It was the most repulsive evening. Judy, determined not to yield an inch to Clara, kept up a gay and cheerful chatter over supper, to which neither Miss Rose nor Clara made any answer whatsoever. As soon as her last mouthful of food was finished, Clara nodded at Miss Rose.

"Clear the table and wash up."

Judy jumped to her feet.

"I'll help. Time you had a holiday, Clara."

Clara turned with apparent politeness to Miss Rose. "Would you like Judy to help?"

Miss Rose, who was nervously shovelling the plates together, shook her head.

"No. No. I prefer to do it alone."

Judy was in two minds whether to agree to this ridiculous situation, then she decided that really it was kinder to Miss Rose to leave her to herself. Tackling her troubles for her probably fussed the old pet. She went upstairs and fetched Mrs. Edwards' letter.

Ever since Judy had been in the house the immensity of hard work that Clara had got through had been a marvel. Up first thing in the morning, to bed late at night, there never seemed to be a moment when she had not found something about the house which needed doing. One of her favourite sayings was, "Other people may have time to sit down, but it's more than I have." It was, therefore, a shock to Judy when she came down the stairs to see through the half-open drawing-room door Clara in Mrs. Former's arm-chair. Not the usual Clara, stiff of back, with a piece of sewing in her hand, but a Clara lolling with her legs stretched out straight in front of her. She looked up as Judy came in and slid further into the chair.

"Surprised to see me resting?"

"Well, it's not like you. It certainly won't do you any harm."

"That's what I think." She took the envelope Judy held out. "From Mrs. Edwards, I suppose." She read it through. "Can't you get into The Bull while they're waiting for a new billet? It should be handy for you, I should think."

Judy was not going to be led into an argument on that point.

"I'll see what can be done. Anyway, Mrs. Edwards will have somewhere for me by next week."

"I should hope so. After all, my aunt is not as young as she was and she's been through a shock."

Judy, eyeing the new Clara, wandered round the room. Would it be the faintest use asking her what she was up to? Why, apparently in a day, everything in the house had changed? Why Miss Rose, who now owned everything, seemed suddenly to have become a slave?

Then out of the window she saw Desmond. It was impossible to hold a sane conversation with Desmond, but might he, in his inconsequent way, let some little clue drop? It was worth trying.

Desmond was sitting under a tree playing with an extremely decayed bird. Judy took the bird from him and threw it into some long grass.

"You mustn't touch that, it's not nice."

Desmond looked at the spot where the bird had fallen.

"I had a fish in a box went bad like that once."

Judy was thankful to find the child sticking to a topic of conversation.

"Things do go bad," she agreed, "if you keep them long enough." Desmond got up and began searching in the long grass where Judy had thrown his bird. Judy called him back. "Come on, leave it alone. I'll play a game with you if you like."

Desmond seemed not to hear what she said. He went on grubbing in the grass, and at the same time singing in a high, tuneless voice. Presently he found his bird, he held it by one leg and returned to Judy. She spoke severely.

"If you bring that horrid thing here I shall only throw it away again."

The child sat down. He spoke as if he were repealing a nursery rhyme.

"Everything belongs to Desmond. Desmond can have anything he likes. Everybody has to do what Desmond says."

Judy gaped at him.

"Good gracious, Desmond! What a way to talk! Everything does not belong to Desmond, in fact nothing here does, it belongs to your great-aunt. Desmond can't have everything he likes, specially he can't have maggoty birds because maggots make Judy sick. And nobody has to do what Desmond says. Children do what grown-up people say, and I tell you to give that bird to me or, for probably the first time in your life, you'll know what it feels like to be smacked."

Desmond swung the bird to and fro like the pendulum of a clock.

"Everything belongs to Desmond. Desmond can have everything he likes. Everybody has to do what Desmond says."

Judy got to her feet.

"All right, my son, you asked for it and you shall have it. Just come to the other side of this tree where dear Mummy can't see you from the window, and then you shall learn what discipline is like." Judy had been brought up on the principle that no child should be punished unless it clearly understood what it was being punished for. Desmond, gazing at the sky and swinging his disgusting bird, had clearly not got his mind on punishment. Judy dragged him behind a good thick laurel, then, keeping her nose as far from the bird as possible, she knelt down so as to bring her face near to Desmond's. "I am going to spank you, Desmond, because I told you to throw away that bird and you haven't. Have you understood?"

Desmond gazed at the bird.

"There's a maggot dropped off him."

Judy snatched at the bird and flung it on to the top of the laurel, and at the same time pulled Desmond across her knee and gave him three firm smacks on his behind. Then she pulled him up straight.

"Now, why did I spank you?"

It would not have surprised Judy what the child answered. She hoped that he realized that he had been punished because he deserved it. Desmond surprised her. He made no protest at the spanking to which she was sure he was totally unused, but regarded her with almost a gleam of intelligence.

"Because of dirty old bird."

"For goodness' sake run away. If you stay here one minute longer I shall spank you for all the times that you've answered rubbish when you could have answered sense." Then a thought struck her. "Why did you kick your Great-aunt Rose?"

Desmond was staring at the top of the laurel.

"Old bird on the top of a tree. Old bird on the top of a tree."

Judy tried to turn him to face her.

"Why did you kick your great-aunt?"

It was clear there was no further sane conversation to be had from Desmond. He wriggled away from her and danced off singing some strange rigmarole about a mouse.

Lady Parsons with Scylla and Charybdis on either side of her was sitting on a plush seat in the lounge of The Bull.

"My dear children, I can't possibly get up because the inn says that dogs shouldn't run about the hotel. Hotel indeed! Just a little country inn, and what could be nicer than a country inn? Why call yourself an hotel when you're not?"

Nicholas kissed his mother.

"But, my lamb, why bring Scylla and Charybdis?"

Lady Parsons gave Judy a woman-to-woman look. "Isn't that exactly like a man? Taking it for granted that Dibble won't mind being left with two dogs on top of everything else. As a matter of fact, it was not at all easy for me to get away. Dibble said, 'It's not that I'm complaining, my lady, nor would wish to stand in Mr. Nick's way, but there's a nasty creak on the top stair which is not accounted for by human feet, and though I'll put up with it without complaint when you're in the house, I couldn't seem to fancy it on my own'."

"What are you going to do with Scylla and Charybdis if they mayn't walk about the inn?" Judy asked.

"Carry them and sit them on the sofas. It only says walk, not sit, on the notice." She turned to Nicholas. "What a funny little bedroom, Nick, and where are you going to sleep, may I ask, while I'm in it?"

Nicholas picked up Scylla.

"Come up to the room and I'll see if I can make more space for you. I expect there are too many of my things about, which makes the room seem smaller than it is." Inside the bedroom Lady Parsons sat on the bed. She turned an eager face to Nicholas.

"Now, what is all this? Why am I here? What good work do you want me to do?"

Nicholas sat down by his mother.

"When Judy and I came up to you for the week-end I told you that I didn't like Judy's billet, that I thought there was something queer about the granddaughter by marriage of the owner. Well, since then the owner's died and both Judy and I are very uneasy about her death, and about the death of the husband, old Mr. Former, which happened some time ago, and about the death of the dog. The doctor, who's also uneasy, has held a post-mortem on old Mrs. Former and he can't find anything the matter, but nobody's satisfied and we all want to get Mrs. Former's daughter, Miss Rose Former, out of the house."

Lady Parsons sighed, and played with one of Charybdis' ears.

"I do hope she will get on with Dibble. Shall I have to keep her for long? And when will she be ready to travel? You couldn't have asked me to come at a more awkward moment, because it seems there's being a census taken of the lectures that all the W.V.S. housewives have been through, and I know I've let some people slip by that I ought not to have done, and I should like to get the whole situation cleaned up before the training officer looks into things too closely." Nicholas glanced at Judy.

"Tell Mother about the new snag."

Judy leant on the rail at the foot of the bed and told Lady Parsons about the events of yesterday evening. Without being aware of it, her fear and disgust at the atmosphere in the house came out in her voice. When she had finished, Lady Parsons held out a hand to her.

"Come here, my child. This is nonsense, you know. All the courage in the world should not make a child of your age stop on in a house like that."

Judy opened her mouth to argue, but Lady Parsons stopped her.

"No, don't argue with me. I know what you're going to say, but I know what I'm going to say. I can stay till next Monday and not a day longer, and on Monday your Miss Rose will travel with me. I shall arrange it."

"But how?" Judy asked. "You see, she won't speak to me. I haven't got the faintest idea what Clara's holding over her. Miss Rose is a silly old pet and almost any bit of nonsense will do, but this is more than some little thing. She must have frightened her into fits in some way, otherwise why should she change all in a moment into a humble, cowed creature doing exactly what Clara tells her?"

Lady Parsons' voice was comfortingly firm.

"I've no idea what this very unpleasant sounding Mrs. Roal can be up to, but I'm accustomed to having my own way. I shall see Miss Rose. From the sound of the story I think probably the doctor could arrange that for me. I'll have a talk with him. Please fix that, Nicholas. Now, what are your immediate plans? When this Miss Rose is out of the house and we've found Judy somewhere else to live, are you going to let the matter rest?" Nicholas gave the hand he was holding an affectionate pat.

"Not on your life! Would you?"

"Certainly not," agreed Lady Parsons. "Apart from the fact that I always did hate seeing people get away with things, it's a bit exciting to be mixed up in a murder. It's like shipwrecks and being left on desert islands; something you read about but never expect to happen to you."

Nicholas got up and began walking up and down the room.

"Judy and I are going to London on Saturday to see the incident officer who looked after the chemist's shop when it was bombed. There might be a clue in what was saved there."

"If there is a clue," Judy broke in, "Nick wants me to search for whatever it is in Clara's bedroom."

Lady Parsons looked sympathetic.

"How extraordinarily unpleasant for you. We had a kitchen-maid once who was supposed to have stolen some silver, but I said to my housekeeper, Well, if she did, she'll have to take it with her. I really can't have rummaging in her box, it's so sordid'."

Nicholas had apparently not listened to this sidetracking of the conversation.

"Our other hope is Mr. Joseph Bloomfield. Doctor Mead says he's sure he's heard the name somewhere." He broke off. "I rather think I'll go and ring him now and fix about your seeing him, and see if his memory has stirred at all."

When the door had shut on Nicholas, Lady Parsons got up off the bed and went to the mirror to tidy her hair. She made a face in the glass.

"Aren't men extraordinary? What woman would put up with a bedroom for months on end in which you can't see a thing in the glass. Where's Nick sleeping? He looks most shockingly tired."

Judy explained about the outhouse and how it had become untenable.

"I'm very afraid he doesn't sleep much. He carries his ground-sheet about, I believe, but that's not a lot of use."

"Well, dear, he wouldn't sleep much if he was in his bed here. In fact, I shan't sleep much myself thinking of you in that house with that unpleasant creature though I know that Nick is within call. Like so many delicate people, you know, he's able to stand any amount more than one would suspect. My Lionel, who was immensely strong, could not miss even a day's sleep without going all to pieces. I do so hope the boy's being sensibly brought up."

Judy spoke without thinking.

"His boy! But I never knew . . ."

"Yes, dear, he married. She's French, a refugee over here. Lionel never told us about the marriage, we only knew when his will was found, and then Nick went to see her and she said she was having Lionel's baby. Nicholas didn't feel I should care for her much, but, of course, I shouldn't have allowed that to enter into the question. I should have made myself care for the mother of my grand-child, but as it happens she's refused to see me. I could, of course, press the point, but I understand the child's being brought up all right, if not in the way I should choose, so there's been no need to interfere."

Judy was full of pity. How sickening for Lady Parsons! What a difference it would make if she had a child of Lionel's to take an interest in! Because she could not think of anything else to say, yet felt she must say something, she said gently:

"How odd, I never knew about the little boy."

"If there hadn't been one Nick would have succeeded to the title." Lady Parsons sighed. "I expect everything's for the best, but I should have liked that. However, when Nick marries perhaps I shall be allowed to see something of his children. At least I hope so."

She said these last words so obviously in a questioning way that Judy flushed. Why on earth did Nick's mother so misjudge her son? Why did she think he was in love with her? If only she could see the casual, friendly, almost brotherly way in which Nicholas regarded her. Because she liked Lady Parsons so much she felt she must disillusion her.

"You mustn't think that Nick is fond of me . . ." Lady Parsons swung round in her chair.

"Mustn't I? You know, Judy my child, strictly between ourselves, though I'm perfectly willing to lend a hand in this little affair of yours and Nick's with a murderess, I really wanted an excuse to come down here. You and I must have a little confidential heart-to-heart talk." She put her finger on her lips. "Sssh. I hear Nick coming."

Nicholas flung open the door. His face was excited and his eyes shining. He spoke to Judy.

"Doctor Mead has remembered. Mr. Joseph Bloomfield is the headmaster of a school run on experimental lines for the training of special children. Get out a piece of paper, Judy, and write to him straight away. Doctor Mead says sign the letter 'Rose Former' and have it sent here care of Mother."

Lady Parsons opened her blotter, found a piece of notepaper and pulled out a chair.

"Come on, dear, here's a pen. Now, Nicholas, tell her what to say."

Nicholas leant against the door gazing into space. Judy sat with her pen poised.

"Dear Mr. Bloomfield," Nicholas dictated, "I am writing to you about my great-nephew, Desmond Roal. My father, who died shortly after he wrote to you, made arrangements about your receiving this child in your school. Owing to my father's, and, more recently, my mother's death the matter of Desmond's education has been allowed to drop, but now that I have inherited my parents' money I feel I should take this matter up again, and I would be glad if you could let me know, by return if possible, what the exact arrangements were that you made with my father. I would be grateful if you would reply in the enclosed stamped addressed envelope as I expect my father told you there is some slight difficulty with the boy's mother, and before he is sent to you I may need to exercise a little tact and persuasion. Yours sincerely, Rose Former."

CHAPTER XVI

AT ONE of the wall tables of the Apéritif in Jermyn Street Judy sat beside Nicholas. She was so happy that the world around her seemed to have changed. Faces were prettier or more handsome, lights were brighter, the jokes at the theatre funnier, the stage dresses gayer. Just a little heightened effect everywhere, and all because she was spending an evening in London with Nicholas. Yet not all because of that. There had not been a chance for much conversation alone with Nicholas' mother, but the few words she had said were enough to lift her spirits over the hills and far away. "Nick is in love with you, my dear. He's a poor gormless idiot with an inferiority complex, so it's up to you to make him speak up, and if he can't, you'll have to do the proposing yourself." A smile curved the corner of Judy's mouth as she remembered this conversation. If Nicholas loved her he had indeed a funny way of showing it. All the way up in the train he discussed Clara Roal. In the intervals in the theatre he discussed Clara Roal. She had no doubt that now, over supper, he would discuss Clara Roal. It was lucky that Clara had no idea of how she was monopolizing Nicholas or it would give her a great deal of pleasure, and that would be more than Judy could bear.

Nicholas finished ordering the food and drink and turned to Judy.

"What are you thinking about?"

For one glorious moment Judy toyed with telling him the truth, repeating the whole of her thoughts, including what Lady Parsons had said, but she had not the courage. Lifted like this into a shimmering world, even though it were perhaps make-believe, was something worth having. It would be frightful if she said, "Your mother says you're in love with me," and Nicholas answered, "Mother's always full of fancies. She's a dear old ass." Quite likely it was all fancy, but if so she did not want to know it to-night. To-night she was in love with Nicholas and imagined Nicholas was in love with her. A gay dream night, not to be spoilt. She took the cigarette he offered her.

"I was thinking of poor old Miss Rose alone with that horror, Clara."

"But she's safe as houses. Clara's plainly got her where she wanted, she has her house and her money, and even the poor old thing working for her. There's no one whose death Clara would dread more."

"If only I could get her to speak to me, if I could find out what Clara was holding over her."

"If Mother can't get a word in edgeways, then nobody can. Mother, as she says herself, is used to having her own way."

"I expect Doctor Mead is right and it's better for him simply to fetch Miss Rose on Monday morning than to try and force things before they're ready. There's no point in making Clara suspicious. Oh, but I do simply hate having to see Miss Rose treated as she is." Judy shuddered. "You've no idea what it's like, Nick. I suspect I only see a tenth of it, and that when I'm at the factory unmentionable things go on. It wouldn't surprise me a bit if Doctor Mead chose to examine her on Monday if he found her bruised from head to foot" Nicholas said nothing for a moment because the waiter was bringing their cocktails. When the man had moved away he turned to Judy. The look in his eyes surprised her by its fierceness.

"Let's drink to our getting a clue from the incident officer to-morrow." He took a sip and spoke in an exasperated voice. "If only that wretched Joseph Bloomfield would answer. I made certain you'd hear by yesterday afternoon's post."

The hors-d'oeuvre wagon was pushed up. There was not really a great deal on it, but to Judy, by the standards of Clara's table, it looked luxurious.

"Don't let's think about the wretched woman any more. Let's make pigs of ourselves while we've got the chance."

Nicholas studied the dishes on the wagon.

"I have to try and remember everything I eat on a jaunt like this. In our guard-room when we're on Home Guard duty we like to hear about each other's trips abroad. We don't often hear about a trip to London. We're very naughty nineties in Pinlock, in our attitude to London. We never go there without expressing what we did with digs in the ribs and winks."

Judy bit a radish in half.

"I must say on this occasion digs in the ribs and winks are very fitting. Shocking, really, what an orgy of vice you and I have been in for."

Nicholas was apparently attending to the hors-d'oeuvre which were being put on his plate.

"The evening's not over yet. You've no idea how terrific the rest of it may be going to be."

They were away from Clara at last and Judy was determined that they should keep away.

"Your mother told me about your nephew. What's the mother like?"

Nicholas ate a sardine before he answered.

"She's one of those boot-button-eyed French women who look as if everything about them snapped. She's very young and, in her way, very good-looking."

"Where did Lionel meet her?"

Nicholas shrugged.

"In the park, on the top of a bus, I don't know. She came over as a refugee and was working at something or other to do with the Free French. She made Lionel happy though. They had a funny sort of domesticated time, which I can understand him wanting. The war makes you feel rather detached and futureless, doesn't it? He married her because of the baby."

"Why won't she see your mother?"

"Lionel wanted her to take the baby to Mother. It's the heir, of course, since Lionel's death. Though he didn't know the baby was coming into that I think he thought that Mother would be a better hand at bringing up the kid than Marcelle, but Marcelle is one of those possessive women, and the end of it all has been she's refused to see Mother at all or let her see the boy. The child is, in fact, being brought up lower middle-class French. However, none the worse for that, I dare say. My hope is that Marcelle will marry again. She's good-looking and attractive in some ways, and she cares nothing for being her ladyship."

"And if she did, your mother would bring up the boy?"

"Not on your life. I don't believe in old people bringing up children. I should adopt him myself."

"And bring him up with your children?"

There was silence for quite a while. When Nicholas spoke he sounded aloof. As if Judy had pried where she had no right.

"That particular point hardly arises. I haven't got many little toddlers sitting round my hearth at the moment. If I ever should have children, then Lionel's boy will join them, if Marcelle should agree."

"Have you spoken to Marcelle about it?"

"No. It's all too problematical. I'm not in a position to make a proposition involving the future."

Judy put down her knife and fork and felt she did not want to eat any more. Quite suddenly the glow faded from the evening. What did Nicholas mean? Why wasn't he in a position to make a proposition involving the future? She glanced at his fine-drawn face and his thin hands. Why did he know Doctor Mead so intimately? Was there something the matter with him? It was as if this thought put all her friendship with Nicholas into focus. His casual keeping her at a distance. An ill man without a future would do that.

His ignoring of over-fatigue. How often had she said to him lately, "You can't go on missing sleep night after night," to which he had answered something vague about one could only die once.

Judy, though she made a manful effort, could not get back into her gay mood. Nicholas was a wonderfully sensitive companion, aware of shades of feeling almost as if he were a woman. He carried on a cheerful chatter and did not seem to mind that all he got from Judy was an occasional yes or no. Then suddenly, when the waiter asked if they would have coffee, he said no, he would have his bill, and turned to her.

"I'm taking you home, my little babbling brook. It can't be good for any woman to chatter so much as you have in the last half-hour."

"I'm sorry. Have I been dull?"

One of her hands was lying on the seat between them. He slipped his over hers.

"You could be a thousand things, Judy, my pet, but dull, never. Come on. I'll take you to your cousin in Kensington and then you'll be fresh for to-morrow." Then he added with one of his odd, shy smiles. "You know, there are such a lot of things that you think, and I know that you think, that I'd like to talk to you about, but, in my opinion, this world is a sad and hard enough place for each one of us without our deliberately adding to each other's burdens." Then, to prevent her picking up his serious tone, he added, "I hope you're full of fortitude, my little lioness, for if I know anything of Jermyn Street on a Saturday night there won't be a smell of a taxi and we'll have to leg it for Kensington."

Nicholas' friend in the Civil Defence Service had arranged that the incident officer who had been in charge when the Roals' shop was bombed, and the two wardens who had worked with him, should be at their Post on Sunday morning. The Post was in South-East London and Nicholas and Judy travelled there on the top of a bus. Nicholas was in tremendous spirits, but Judy had slept badly and found this hard to disguise. All night in her dreams she had been haunted by disasters. As is the way of dreams, not all the disasters happened to Nicholas, sometimes it was disasters to herself, but always there was a feeling of things going wrong and her happiness being ruined. She had wakened up in tears.

The Wardens' Post was three rooms in a partially blitzed school. Judy and Nicholas were greeted by the Post Warden, who introduced them to the incident officer and the two other wardens.

"This is Mr. Smithers, my deputy, he was incident officer on the particular incident in which you are interested. This is Joe Crawley, who was working with him, and this Nobby Clark, who was acting as messenger from the incident to the Post. They've got the log-book and some papers, and I think you'll find that they'll be able to tell you anything you want to know. There's a room here that you can use for as long as you like. You'll not be disturbed, except that one of our ladies will be making a cup of tea later on and will bring you in a cup."

The room they were given to talk in was bare and formal. There was a table in the middle and some chairs against the wall. Judy's heart sank. They wanted such difficult information, the sort of information which, if the wardens knew it, could probably only be drawn out in long, slow conversation over a mug of beer. The setup of this formal interview seemed to her all wrong, but she had reckoned without Nicholas. In two minutes he had established a friendly attitude.

"I'm terribly sorry to bother you fellows to turn out on a Sunday morning. I'll be as quick as I can, for I know you want to be back on the allotments, but I'm not here to waste your time. You've been told what incident I'm interested in. I'd like to be able to tell you why I'm interested, but I can't do that. The point is that Miss Rest here and myself have come up against something a bit peculiar, and we want you to rack your brains and see what you can remember that might give us a clue. I can just tell you one thing: it's just possible that somebody got hold of some rather dangerous stuff in that chemist's shop, and if you can lend a helping hand now you might be able to save somebody's life." He felt in his pocket and took out a box of cigarettes and some matches. He laid them on the table. "Help yourselves. Now, Mr. Smithers, do you remember the chemist's shop being hit?"

Mr. Smithers was a big man with a red face. He took a cigarette and lit it. He paused before he spoke, clearly marshalling his thoughts.

"It was hit at nineteen hours. We went straight to the incident and it was a bit of a job. We knew Alfred Roal was there and we had quite a job," he glanced at Judy. "No need to go into that, he was killed, you know. The shop was almost entirely wrecked, with the exception of a bit behind the door; there was a cupboard there, everything was pitched out by the blast, but it was not demolished like the rest. We had to prop the place up before we could get out Roal's body. Mrs. Roal was living outside London. We got in touch with friends of hers and they told her. Must have rung her up, I think, for she came to the incident very early on, didn't she, Joe?"

Joe was a perky little man with blue eyes.

"That's right. As soon as it was light. Mr. Fothergill, up the street, had let her know; he was a china of Roal's."

Nicholas looked sympathetic.

"I suppose she was in a terrible state, poor thing?"

Joe nodded.

"Shocking. She stood outside what had been the shop and kept staring at it, saying over and over again stuff about saving the place and how it was all they had; didn't seem to take in what she was looking at really. We did what we could, asked her if she wouldn't like to go along to the Rest Centre for a bit of breakfast, but no, we couldn't make her budge. They're often like that, you know. Seems as if they'd got to stand and stare. I told Nobby here to pop back to the Post and see if there was a mobile canteen coming along; we thought a cup of tea might do her good. There was no way of making one, for all the heat had gone in that area."

Nobby broke in. He was a skinny, grey little man. He spoke quickly, his words tumbling over each other.

"I run back and told the Post Warden and he told one of our ladies to get on the phone and find when the mobile was coming our way. When I came back to the incident Mrs. Roal had gone into the shop, or into what there was of it, and was carrying on like a madwoman, digging about amongst the soot and that on the floor and moaning. Looked very rough she did."

Nicholas turned to Mr. Smithers.

"What did she take away?"

Mr. Smithers opened an exercise book.

"I've got my report here. Of course the stuff all belonged to her. We knew her and it was all right for her to touch anything she wanted to, but you have to check up in a case like that because there was quite a lot of stuff thrown out of the shelves and, of course, we had to be careful because of looting. I'd made a sort of rough list before she came. There was soap, and some blue-paper bundles that might have been cotton wool, a few sponges and stuff in boxes; it was all in a bad way, you know, mixed up with soot and rubble. You couldn't rightly tell what was what. She took some of all sorts. She pushed some of it into her bag and a lot more she rolled up in a jersey coat that she was wearing. She had pulled off her overcoat, and taken off her jersey and piled the stuff on it, kind of frenzy she was in, really. I came and stood by her, trying to check what she was taking and at the same time to get her to see reason. I told her we'd put everything safe for her and the best thing she could do was to let Joe take her round to the Rest Centre, but she was like a mad thing, she couldn't seem to hear what was said. Then up she got off her knees, dragged on her overcoat and, with the stuff she'd picked up carried in her jersey as if it were a bag, she started running up the road."

"Just as the W.V.S. canteen came round the corner," Joe put in.

Judy smiled.

"I expect you were glad of a cup of tea though."

"You've said it," Joe agreed. "Cup of hot cocoa I had and a couple of good sandwiches. Written on the canteen was that it was a gift of New York. Raining cats and dogs it was, didn't half bless little old New York that morning."

Nicholas glanced at Mr. Smithers' note-book.

"Was much stuff saved?"

Mr. Smithers turned over a page. He cleared his throat.

"Eighty-two cakes of soap miscellaneous. Fourteen sponges very soiled. Two eye-baths. Three cardboard boxes containing ampoules of injections. Seven ampoules smashed. Eighteen boxes of paper handkerchiefs. One bottle of hair oil."

Nicholas was making notes on a piece of paper.

"And Mrs. Roal had taken what?"

"Some more cakes of soap, the blue packets, some sponges and a few of the boxes, and some oddments in bottles. I rather think there was a bottle of salts."

"Did the boxes that Mrs. Roal took hold the same as the boxes of injections that you salvaged?"

Mr. Smithers nodded.

"Just the same. I reckon Mr. Roal kept that particular stuff in one place."

Nicholas managed to speak calmly.

"What were the injections? You don't happen to know that, I suppose?"

Mr. Smithers turned over another page of his exercise book.

"Yes, I do. Mr. Perkins, he's another chemist, he came to look over the stuff and I got what he said here. 'Mr. Perkins called at the Post at sixteen hours, he came to ask about Roal's stuff with a view to making Mrs. Roal an offer for what was saved. He said we ought to put the injection stuff somewhere safe where it wouldn't get knocked about. He said it was stuff for asthma and to stop bleeding. It was called Adrenalin'."

CHAPTER XVII

LADY Parsons was waiting for Judy and Nicholas in the lounge of The Bull. On a table in front of her were two cocktails. She nodded at them with pride.

"I've bought you both a cocktail. The gin seemed to be giving out, so I thought I'd better have them ready as you were sure to be tired." She lowered her voice. "And, of course, I wanted to keep a table. Now don't keep me waiting. What did you find out? The moment I got your telephone message I got on to Doctor Mead. He'll be here to supper. Oh, I forgot." She opened her bag and took out an envelope. "The letter's come; nobody will ever know what I've endured not opening it. I so wanted to open it this afternoon that I had to take Scylla and Charybdis for an immense walk to keep my mind off it. They tried to catch a squirrel, and they are both exhausted and asleep on my bed."

Judy opened the envelope. It was a big envelope and there were a number of papers inside. The one on the top started "Dear Miss Former". Nicholas gave her hand a pat.

"Go on, don't be a meany, read it out aloud."

"Dear Miss Former," Judy read, "I am so glad to hear from you. Yes, your father did intend to send his great-grandson to me. You will see from the enclosed correspondence why he chose this school, but actually I learnt more of his reasons by word of mouth. You are evidently not aware that some time before his death your father met me in London. He told me he was not much of a hand at letter-writing and he found it easier to talk. From what he told me of your great-nephew I felt he was a child I could help. My school is for backward and difficult children who are quite unsuited to ordinary forms of education. Desmond was to be put under my sole charge for at least two years, during which time you were to decide if I were the right person to train him. If he proved suitable I should then keep him until he was old enough to be placed in some profession. My aim, in which I may say I have been very successful, is to fit the boys and girls given into my care to take a more or less normal place in the world. If you consider sending Desmond to me I should be very glad if you would come over to see us and see my work. I quite understand about the mother. Your father had explained this difficulty to me and it is one which I am very used to handling. Yours sincerely, Joseph Bloomfield."

Nicholas picked up the other letters which were enclosed. They were dated over some months. He glanced at Judy.

"Shall I read these?" She nodded. The letters were creased with much reading. He smoothed them flat and put them in order. "The first is from Mr. Former. 'Dear Sir, I am a Mason and I have heard through a fellow Mason of your establishment and would be grateful for all particulars, having under my care a boy about whose mental state I am not satisfied.' To that Mr. Joseph Bloomfield has enclosed a copy of his reply, simply saying that he encloses a printed book about his school and could Mr. Former come and see him, and what age is the boy." Nicholas laid the two letters aside and opened a third. "Mr. Former was evidently right in saying that he was not much of a hand at writing, for this one simply gives the date of Desmond's birth and says thanks for the enclosure of the 27th inst. Then I think there must have been a letter from Mr. Joseph Bloomfield missing because this last one is from Mr. Former again. 'Dear Sir, In reply to yours received yesterday, I beg to inform you that I will be in London on Wednesday, the 18th, as you suggest, and will meet you in the lounge of the Grosvenor Hotel, Victoria, at twelve noon'."

Nicholas folded the letters and passed them back to Judy. "He sounds rather a nice old boy, old Former."

Judy looked down at Joseph Bloomfield's letter.

"I like the sound of Mr. Bloomfield. I wonder if he could have done anything with Desmond if he'd had him. I wouldn't wonder a bit if he could. I'm perfectly certain that he needn't be anything like he is."

Lady Parsons tapped on the table with her fingers.

"I've been very patient, dears. Will you now please tell me what you discovered in London? What was the woman seen carrying away from the ruins? Was it arsenic?"

Nicholas got to his feet.

"Here's Doctor Mead. We know what she took away, but we haven't the faintest idea whether it's the answer. Here's the man to tell us that."

Because the bar was getting crowded they went into the dining-room and sat at a corner table which was set well apart from the others. Nicholas ordered Doctor Mead a drink and told Judy to give him Mr. Bloomfield's letters.

"You might read those," he said. "It hitches on to what Judy and I have got to say."

The waitress seemed to take an unconscionable time taking their order and bringing their food, but as soon as she had put their meat in front of them, Judy, unable to hold back her question any longer, almost hurled it at the doctor.

"Could Mrs. Former and Mr. Former and Mr. Jones have died of injections of adrenalin?"

Doctor Mead had face muscles trained to resist shock. Years of leaning over patients and seeing signs of a hitherto unexpected disease had taught him to speak casually and soothingly, while his mind worked furiously on known facts and so far unconsidered trends. He did just that at this moment. He was faced with what to him, as a doctor, was an appalling suggestion. He it was who had, as it were, put the hypodermic into Clara's hands, he it was who with just a grain of dissatisfaction had signed Mr. Former's death certificate. He it was who had watched the post-mortem on Mrs. Former with a dim knowledge of what he was looking for. Adrenalin! An overdose of that! He would have to go into the subject more closely, but surely it was undetectable? Why had he never thought of it? Because, of course, no ordinary person would be in possession of sufficient quantities of adrenalin to give a lethal injection without the knowledge of their doctor. His face, however, looked unmoved and his voice was unexcited.

"Adrenalin. Well, we must look into that. There might be possibilities there."

Nicholas grinned at him.

"Now then, you old professional, no bedside manner with us. Could you, or couldn't you, kill a person with an overdose of adrenalin?"

Doctor Mead sipped the glass of sherry at his side. His eyes twinkled at Nicholas.

"You're a professional yourself, my boy. If I were to spring a question upon you at this moment as to how much explosive we should need to blow up the whole Bigfields factory, you wouldn't snap out and tell me off hand, there'd be a lot of humming and hawing. Tell you the truth, I don't know the exact answer about adrenalin. I'm absolutely sure that you could inject a lethal dose to kill, but I'm not sure how detectable it would be in that quantity."

Judy startled them all. She gave a little gasp and her hands clutched the edge of the table. Her face had turned white.

"Oh, goodness! I must have helped to murder Mrs. Former."

Doctor Mead gave her a professional glance. His voice was rough but comforting.

"If it comes to that, my dear girl, I must have helped to murder people ever since I took my Hippocratic oath. The little slip there, and the little mistake here, and the blind unenlightened ignorance that, I regret to say, has dogged me all my life. I'm probably responsible for a nice row of stones in the churchyard by now."

Nicholas was sitting on Judy's right. He gave her hand a squeeze under the table.

"Don't look like that, you old idiot. It's not like you to dramatize yourself."

Judy nodded, but she was still appalled at what she could see in her mind. She spoke slowly, recalling what had happened incident by incident.

"It was still light. Clara had given Mrs. Former sleeping stuff in some soup and when we came upstairs the old lady was drowsy, too drowsy to mind who gave her the injection. We made the bed and washed her. The tray with the injections was on the window-ledge. There was the insulin and the syringe; the syringe was in bits and the needle was detached and they were all lying in a jar of cotton wool soaked in surgical spirit."

"Who put the syringe together?" Doctor Mead asked.

"Clara. Very neatly, in an experienced sort of way."

Doctor Mead was watching Judy's face.

"You actually saw her draw the insulin into the syringe?"

Judy nodded.

"Yes. Twenty units."

Nicholas' voice was eager.

"And then what happened?"

Judy turned to him.

"Yes, you're quite right, that's where I've been wrong all the time. Clara sent me to strip back the sheets and asked me to dab a little bit of spirit above Mrs. Former's knee, and in that time she could have squirted the insulin out of the window and refilled the syringe with adrenalin." Her voice trembled a little. "I watched the needle go in and I saw Clara take it out and tuck the old lady up. Then she went away. She said she would draw the curtains because of the morning light. She laid the syringe on the tray and in the most ordinary way in the world asked me to take it apart and put it back in the spirit. How easy it was for her! Fancy making me an accomplice! Oh, haven't I been a fool?"

Doctor Mead spoke quite sharply.

"You'll be a fool, my girl, if you dramatize it. If this supposition is correct, and, mind you, it's still a supposition, then she made an accomplice of me. All those stories about the old man complaining of being in a nervous state and getting fanciful. I thought at the time it was very unlike him. If your adrenalin guess is right and she wanted to make me order an injection, then I bet you the old boy was complaining about real things. Probably she moved things on purpose to get on his nerves. When I think of her standing in my surgery looking the picture of innocence, and saying in a low, anxious voice that perhaps she was being unduly fussy, but she was so fond of the old man, and then laughing and saying that she was afraid he was going to be a tiresome patient, that he was just like her husband, never could be persuaded to take a drop of medicine. My word! If we prove that she finished off the old boy I could strangle her with my own hands. It was just like him to take all that trouble to find a modern place for young Desmond. I looked up the history of Bloomfield's school while you've been in town. It wouldn't really have been old Former's cup of tea. It's partly a farm, he'd have liked that, but any amount of handicraft that he'd have thought arty and crafty, and, above all, the cure is based on music; no matter how unmusical the kids are when they come to him he squeezes them into an orchestra and they learn to play a drum or a cymbal or what-not. It's a terrific experiment."

Lady Parsons leant towards him.

"Why should this woman, Roal, have been so against the place? I mean, sufficiently to get rid of her husband's grandfather in order that her boy shouldn't go there."

Doctor Mead laid down his fork and knife.

"I've been considering the question of Clara Roal. The Formers were a talkative old couple. Old Former particularly. He couldn't bear Clara, you know, mainly because she is a clever woman and he detested clever women. I used to put it down as an age prejudice on his part. Now, of course, I can see what a fool I may have been. Like most people who deal with animals, he'd developed an extra sensitivity, and knew for a fact a whole lot of things that he couldn't exactly explain, and, of course, one of the things he may have felt was that there was something queer about Clara. As far as I can remember from what the old people told me, she was the daughter of a greengrocer or something of the sort in Croydon, eldest of six, brilliantly clever, won a scholarship and was never able to take it up because there were all the other kids to look after. But the father was a queer character. Terrific preacher. Jehovah's witness or something of the sort. One of those sort of Christians who think that he's justified in letting the children go short of everything while he's saving other people's souls. But there's a bit of the story missing that I'm sure the old man told me, or at least hinted at. It was either that Clara's father finished in an asylum, or came to a violent end, or proved to be out of his mind. I can't remember."

"Then that would account for Desmond?" said Judy. The Doctor shrugged his shoulders.

"Maybe there's a strain of madness running through the family. If it's proved that Clara took the adrenalin – a very difficult thing to prove, by the way – I should think some queer family history might come to light." The waitress came to the table to clear their plates. Nicholas waited until she had gone and leant forward and lowered his voice.

"Well, what's the next thing? She's got a locked box in her bedroom, that's where she probably keeps the stuff. How are we going to have a look at it?"

"You're not," said Doctor Mead decidedly. "At the present moment, even supposing we're dealing with a madwoman, there's not the slightest danger to anybody, and, mind you, even supposing your guess is correct, I don't consider she is mad in the sense of not knowing what she's doing. Miss Rose, though she doesn't know it, is being got out of the house to-morrow anyway. Judy can help us by returning home to-night with the news that she's got a new billet." He turned to Judy. "You can explain that Lady Parsons is going and that you're moving into The Bull. If Judy starts to pack tonight Clara will feel that everything's coming her way, and when I pop by to-morrow to get Miss Rose into my car it won't be so difficult. Tonight I think you and I have got a job to do, Nick. Even though we're dealing with little more than a suspicion, it's time we told the police; it's their business to decide whether a search ought to be made of Clara's room. We'll pop along and see them after dinner."

Nicholas looked worried.

"I simply hate Judy going up there by herself."

The Doctor nodded.

"I see your point. Well, she's got some luggage, I suppose, a case or something; suppose, Judy, that you say quite frankly that Nick's going to leave it later on, and when he leaves it he can stay on and do his watchdog act – though, mind you, I can't see that she's got anything whatsoever against Judy, particularly as she's leaving."

Lady Parsons gave a little squeak.

"I tell you what, I'll walk back with Judy. I've got to take Scylla and Charybdis for a little run anyway, and I'll say myself that I'm leaving to-morrow and that Judy's moving into my room. Incidentally, I don't mind confessing I shall be delighted at the opportunity, I dare say it's morbid of me, but I should like to have just one look at that unpleasant creature, Clara."

Lady Parsons and Judy stood on the steps of The Bull and watched Nicholas and the doctor drive away, then Lady Parsons took Judy's arm.

"There! I'm a clever old woman. I was determined to get you to myself. Has Nick said anything?"

Judy hesitated. Could she tell Nicholas' mother what Nicholas had said? Suppose Nicholas was ill, there was no reason why Lady Parsons should know about it. She had suffered enough already in this war without that anxiety clutching at her. Then something about Lady Parsons' face made her change her mind. Courage was written in every line of it. She was not a woman who flinched from knowing the truth.

"I'll tell you exactly what he said. It was not said about me, but just about marrying. 'It's all too problematical. I'm not in a position to make a proposition involving the future.' I'd always known he was delicate, but . . ."

Lady Parsons shouted to Scylla who was loitering. "Come on, you bad dog, how often have I told you not to hang about in the middle of the road? Nick isn't ill. He was completely overhauled at the time of his registration; he's not fit to be a Commando or anything like that, he's just not robust, that's all." She walked a moment or two in silence, thinking. "What work does Nick do?"

Judy again hesitated. Nicholas had carefully not told his mother what work he did, so presumably he did not want her to know.

"Something or other to do with shells."

Lady Parsons took Judy's arm.

"Don't be tiresome, dear. I'm not a child. What does he do?"

"Well, I wouldn't know for certain. He never talks about it, but it must be something to do with special explosives because where he works isn't just covered with grass, but, as well, he's got a blast-proof wall around him. They say in the factory that if what he's working on comes off it'll make Hitler eat all the carpets in Germany – at least that's how a setter put it."

"Well, now, can't a mother be an idiot! And all this time I thought Nick wouldn't talk about his work because he was ashamed at having to do a civilian job, and that explains why, when he introduced me the night before last to one of the directors of the factory, the director said to me he supposed I must be very proud." She turned to Judy with a smile extraordinarily like Nicholas' own, "And that explains why a man who's head over ears in love won't ask the girl he loves to marry him."

"He couldn't be such a fool. Even if I knew everything was going wrong and the stuff he's working on was going to blow him to pieces in three weeks' time, I'd marry him. After all, in these times you're very lucky to have even two or three weeks' happiness."

"There's a bit more to it than that. Being in love is one thing, being man and wife is another. You don't know how the constant anxiety might wear you down. You see, you feel different about a man when he's yours. That, I think, is what Nick is afraid of for you."

"But I'm not afraid of it for myself. I should think he might give me the chance to make up my own mind." They were at the corner of the road. Lady Parsons had a double lead; she called Scylla and Charybdis and clipped the lead to their collars.

"Better not have the dogs digging over the place, the Roal creature might be annoyed enough to give them a dose of adrenalin." She straightened up and laid a hand on Judy's shoulder. "If you want your happiness, my girl, ask for it. You look Nick in the eye, forget all about Leap Year and that sort of rubbish, and if he tries to argue, talk him down." She drew Judy to her and gave her a kiss. "Your marriage would give me a great deal of pleasure. I rather thought lately that I'd closed the door on personal happiness, but if I had you for a daughter-in-law I think I might see a little of it stealing back. Come on now, let's go and have a look at your murderess."

Clara was sitting in a chair on the lawn. Not, this time, upright and sewing, but lolling, her eyes on the sky. Lady Parsons did not wait for a formal introduction.

"Forgive my intruding on you, but I've only just walked up from the inn with Judy. I've been staying here to see something of my son, Nicholas Parsons, whom I think you've met. This naughty girl has made me cut my time here short, she is moving into my room tomorrow."

Clara made no pretence that she was not delighted. "Good. This place is not at all suitable for Judy. It's too lonely, and it's been rather a sad house lately, and, to be honest, with a small boy and a rather incompetent great-aunt, I've got my hands full."

Lady Parsons sat down without being invited.

"I'm sure you have. Looking after people is such a nuisance. What a pretty place you have here! What lovely roses! That's a Madame Herriot climbing up the house, isn't it? What a late flowerer!"

Clara, pleased at the thought of Judy's departure, was unusually gracious. She turned to Judy.

"Take the scissors out of my work-basket in the drawing-room, Judy, and pick a few buds. You can reach them from the window in the passage."

Judy went into the house. She collected the scissors, ran into her bedroom and threw her coat, hat and bag on the bed, then she went to the passage window. That window had unpleasant memories for her; it was there she had stood with Clara on the night of Mrs. Former's death, and heard Clara gloat over the loneliness of the place. There were several buds within reach, and she leant out and picked a handful. Clara's and Lady Parsons' voices came to her. Then she heard another sound behind her; she turned and saw Miss Rose pressed against the wall.

Miss Rose's appearance shocked Judy. Her face looked puffy and unhealthy, and there were streaks of tears on her cheeks. She spoke in a frightened voice.

"Oh, Judy, I heard what that lady said to Clara. You're leaving to-morrow."

Judy thought quickly. Was it wise to tell Miss Rose what was planned for her? She was silly and she was frightened, and might easily give away what she was thinking.

"It's all right, darling. I know exactly what I'm doing. You can trust me, can't you?"

"But you said you were going."

"I know, darling, but you'll just have to trust me that there's nothing for you to worry about." She held one of Miss Rose's hands. "What are you letting Clara work you so hard for?"

Miss Rose's manner changed. She tried to draw her hand away.

"Oh, she doesn't! It's just that I wish to work."

Judy gripped her hand more firmly.

"I don't believe a word of it. Come on, you and I have always been friends. What fearful secret has she found out about you?"

It was a shot in the dark, but it struck lucky. Miss Rose's eyes were round with wonder.

"How did you know I had a secret? Did she tell you?"

"No, but I could see that she'd frightened you pretty badly. Come on, what have you been up to?"

Miss Rose looked up at Judy with anxious eyes.

"You would never tell anybody, would you, dear? I wouldn't tell you, but, as you've guessed there's something, you may as well know what it is. Clara says it isn't safe to trust anybody when it's something shocking like this is, but I think I could trust you. You wouldn't go to the police, would you, Judy?"

Judy thought of Nicholas and the doctor at this very moment. She tightened her grip on Miss Rose's hand.

"Come on, darling. Tell me everything, you know perfectly well you can trust me to help."

Miss Rose reduced her voice to the merest breath of sound.

"It started while Mother was alive. What with one thing and another there never seemed to be a great deal to eat. You know how it was, Judy dear. Then one day when I was in the grocer's that nice woman was serving at the provision counter, and she let me have a tin of pilchards." Miss Rose paused and spoke in a gasp. "No points, dear. Well, that wasn't the only time. I got into the way of coming home with little tins. It was very wrong, dear, I see that now. When Mother died I wasn't well, you remember, and Clara came to my room, and why, I don't know, but she opened my cupboard. It happened that there were four tins there: one of sardines that I'd put by for a treat for Mother, two of meat and one of salmon."

Judy was struggling hard to look properly shocked. "And what did Clara say when she found them?"

"Well, at first she said it was her duty to go straight to the police. That I was one of these black-market cases that you read of in the papers, and the punishment was prison, not only for me but for that nice woman at the grocer's. Well, of course, dear, I can't let that woman get into trouble, and I'm afraid for myself; it's the shame, I could never face it." She broke off for a moment. "Oh, Judy, now you know you won't tell, will you? I'm so frightened that I wake up in the night in a bath of perspiration."

Judy turned and peered out of the window to make quite sure that Clara and Lady Parsons were still talking. It was all right. The low murmur of their voices was still going on. She turned back to Miss Rose.

"And then Clara decided not to report you if you did exactly what she told you, including asking me to leave the house?"

"That's right, dear. It was my punishment." Tears rolled down Miss Rose's cheeks. "I know it seems terrible, Judy dear, but you know I didn't realize what I was doing. Of course, I knew that everything had to be on points, but they seemed such little things each time, and that woman at the grocer's was so kind. Somehow until I saw Clara's face I never knew it was what they call black-marketing."

Judy put an arm round her.

"It's all right, darling. A wrong thing to do, but nobody on earth would send you to prison for it." She hesitated, longing to lift a little of the burden of fear off Miss Rose's shoulders. There was to-morrow to think of. It would make Doctor Mead's task of getting Miss Rose out of the house much more difficult if she showed even a shade of change in her behaviour and made Clara suspicious. Far safer after she was away from the house for Lady Parsons to handle the situation. Probably she would suggest something sensible, either a cancellation of present coupons or even a confession to a policeman. Once she was away it should not be difficult to put the old dears fears at rest. She gave Miss Rose a kiss. "Don't cry, darling. Everything's going to be quite all right, I promise you. Now I must take out these roses or Clara will suspect I've been gossiping with you."

Judy walked with Lady Parsons to the gate. Lady Parsons held out her rosebuds.

"Very gracious, wasn't she? She's rather a good-looking creature. You know, Judy, I shall keep one of these rosebuds and press it. It'll be interesting to have as a souvenir of having known a murderess."

Judy shivered.

"I shall be glad when to-night's over. I saw Miss Rose while I was getting the roses." She described what had happened. "When she's with you you could make her see sense about all that, couldn't you?"

Lady Parsons nodded.

"She sounds exactly like Dibble. Once before the war Dibble smuggled half a bottle of brandy into this country. She looked ill for weeks afterwards, and I was just going to get a doctor to her when she confessed. 'Wrapped in that fox fur of yours, my lady. If it had been found it was you who would have got the blame. I have nightmares every night, wake up with the shivers, my lady, seeing them leading you away'."

Judy giggled.

"Did she enjoy the brandy?"

"Oh, dear me, no. She only brought it in to put in her medicine cupboard. She said, 'I like to have it by me, my lady, just in case. Not that I'd ever touch it, but it's nice to know it's there.' I cured her conscience on that occasion by telling her to send a half-crown book of stamps to the Chancellor of the Exchequer. We typed a nice little slip to go with it saying 'conscience money'. Dibble recovered the second that was in the post." They were at the gate. Lady Parsons kissed Judy. "Good night, my dear child. I shouldn't leave you with that horrible woman if I didn't know Nick would be along any minute. Don't forget now what I told you to do. I expect a telegram from you both by at least the day after to-morrow."

Clara was in the kitchen when Judy got back to the house. She was boiling some milk. She sounded unusually cheerful.

"I thought we both might have a cup of cocoa. That's a nice woman, you'd never think her husband had been an earl. She talks just as simply as anybody else. She says I'm quite right to get you moved, it is lonely out here for a girl of your age."

Judy did not really want the cocoa, but it was her last night in the house so she thought it might as well pass pleasantly. She sat down at the table.

"Nick will be up presently with my suit-case."

Clara had put out two cups. She now nodded at the dresser.

"Better get out another cup and saucer then, maybe he'd fancy a cup."

Judy took down the cup and saucer, though she could not imagine Nicholas drinking cocoa. On the other hand he might be amused at drinking it with Clara. Whatever could have come over her to be so generous all of a sudden? Clara was pouring the hot milk into the two cups and stirring in the cocoa. She seemed to read what was in Judy's mind.

"There was some extra milk to-day. It won't keep this weather, I think there's thunder about." She passed Judy her cup. "It's sweetened cocoa, it won't want any sugar."

"That's more like herself," thought Judy. She stirred her cocoa.

"I'm tired. It's a long journey up and back from London. The train was very crowded."

"Did you have a nice time with your cousin?"

Judy sipped her cocoa.

"Yes, and Nick took me to a theatre. It was all very nice really."

"And what did you do this morning?"

Judy went on drinking while she thought of a good answer.

"We had to have rather an early lunch because of the train. We went for a bus ride. London was looking hot and dirty and dusty, we thought, but I suppose it wouldn't be to you; you lived there, didn't you?"

Clara had wandered over to the window with her cup of cocoa in her hand. She was peering down the drive.

"I don't see Mr. Parsons. Funny his coming so late with your luggage."

"He's busy, I suppose," said Judy vaguely. "He'll be along presently." She swallowed the last of her cocoa. "I'll go upstairs and start getting ready for bed. I shall see him coming from the window."

Clara nodded. "That's right. Good night, sleep tight." Judy went up to her room and leant out of the window. Nicholas was late, it was long after ten. The talk with the police must have taken longer than he had expected. It did not matter really; the later he brought the suit-case the sooner it would be dark, and that meant he had not got to go back, but could hide himself in the garden right away. How nice it would be at The Bull to-morrow! Poor Nicholas still would not have anywhere to sleep, but they liked him at The Bull and would probably give him a bed in a bathroom. Could Lady Parsons be right? Did Nick love her? What was it exactly Lady Parsons had said? It was at this point in her thinking that Judy suddenly realized that she was losing her grip on her thoughts and that her eyelids were closing. Good gracious, she thought, I've got most frightfully sleepy all of a sudden. I'd better start getting undressed or I shall go to sleep standing up. Blinking, she went across to her bed and picked up her coat and hat and went across to the wardrobe to put them away. As she reached the wardrobe she stumbled, and as she stumbled she jerked herself out of her drowsiness just sufficiently to think clearly for a moment. Swaying with sleep, the horrid realization crept over her. This was not normal sleepiness. This was drugged sleepiness. Clara must have put something in her cocoa.

Judy's hospital training had included many lectures, and the words of one lecturer came back to her. It was a lecture on narcotic drugs. She could hear the lecturer saying, "Keep the patient moving, walk them about." Judy forced herself to hang up her coat and then turned to her bed, where her bag was lying. "I'll walk downstairs and say I'll meet Nick. I'll walk and I'll walk and I'll walk." Her knees sagged under her and her head lolled forward. She pulled herself together. "Wake up, you fool. Goodness knows why Clara's drugged you, but she has. Go on, open the door, walk down the stairs." She pinched herself. "That's better, that's made you open your eyes, now try and think clearly. What are you going to do? You're going to get out of this house and find Nick." She picked up her bag. "You won't want anything else. Everything you want is in your suitcase." She stood there swaying, repeating stupidly to herself over and over again, "Everything you want is in your suit-case." The thought must have connected in her brain with her bag, because she opened it. Like all women she had a system when filling a bag to see she had forgotten nothing. She repeated this now. "Handkerchief, comb, powder, lipstick, money, handkerchief, comb, powder, lipstick . . ." She broke off, staring at the bag. Surely there ought to be something in it that was not there. Surely she had put something important in it to-night. "Handkerchief, comb, lipstick" Then, through her sleep-sodden brain came a flash of intelligence. The envelope from Joseph Bloomfield. It was gone.

CHAPTER XVIII

IT SEEMED to Judy, swaying and nodding by the side of her bed, that sleep was coming at her in the form of large mattresses. They seemed to pile softly on her, and no sooner had she shaken off one than she was being smothered by another. Between these mattresses of sleep small stabs of reason reached her benumbed brain. Clara had Joseph Bloomfield's letters. Clara knew that she, Judy, had found out something which could connect her with the death of Mr. Former. Clara got rid of people she did not want. Clara must be waiting for her to go to sleep and then she would bring her hypodermic. But Nicholas was coming. Nicholas would be here any minute with her case. She must get downstairs. She must get to Nicholas. But sleep had now got hold of her legs. She seemed to have no control over them, no ability to make them move. The only thing she seemed able to do was to keep herself from lying on the bed. Each time a mattress of sleep overwhelmed her some part of her brain continued to say, "You mustn't lie down, don't lie down."

Between one wave of sleep and another Judy heard the stairs creak. She dug her nails into her arm and forced her eyes open. Clara was coming up. Clara must not be allowed to think the sleeping-draught had over-come her. She was waiting for that moment, but it had not come yet. It must never come. She was startled by a knock on her door. Clara spoke in her normal voice.

"Judy, Judy."

"She thinks I'm asleep," thought Judy. "Now I'll startle her." With a terrific effort she forced herself to answer.

"Yes."

Clara put something down outside the door.

"It's your suit-case. Mr. Parsons has brought it round."

Judy, still keeping herself awake, listened to Clara's retreating footsteps. At the bottom of the stairs Clara spoke again.

"Thank you, Mr. Parsons. Good night"

Judy, struggling hard against unconsciousness, grasped what had happened. Nicholas had brought the case, had not been satisfied at Clara's reply that she was asleep, and had insisted on seeing the suit-case taken up. If only she had not tried so hard to keep awake. He must have heard her voice and been satisfied. She tried to shout, but the one word to Clara seemed to have exhausted her powers in that direction, for her mouth would barely open and all that came through in the way of sound was a confused mumble. It was then she remembered the whistle. The whistle which, since the night when Clara came to her room, she had worn round her neck.

Drugged sleep, Judy discovered, is like an anaesthetic in the coming-round stage. One moment you are in this world seeing and reasoning, and the next you have drifted away again out of reach. Judy, clutching at the bed to steady herself, found her patches of sanity not long enough. The whistle seemed to have caught on a strap, probably of her cami-knickers. She pulled, and then even while she was pulling, forgot what she was trying to do and let her hand slip away from her throat, then in the next patch of sanity it was all to be done over again. But by degrees her need for the whistle became fixed in both her conscious and her subconscious mind. She clawed at the ribbon round her neck and muttered "whistle, whistle" even while sleep had overcome her. In doing so she must have pulled too hard, for suddenly the ribbon broke. She had nothing on but her frock and the cami-knickers; the frock was held in at the waist by a leather belt: undo the belt and the whistle would fall to the floor. It took time for her to reason this and what seemed to be aeons of time to take off her belt. Finally it was accomplished, and with a soft thud the whistle fell on the carpet. Clutching at the bed, she leant forward, struggling through her sleep-dimmed eyes to see it, and at that moment there was another creak on the stairs. Confused as she was with sleep, she felt terror.

"I can't lock the door. I can't lock the door. No furniture to keep her out. She came before. No furniture to keep her out. I must find the whistle. The window's open, Nick would hear me in a moment if I blew it. I must find the whistle. I must find the whistle." Judy was on her knees now, her head nodding, her eyes dimmed, but her hands were patting the carpet. "I must find the whistle, I must find the whistle." At that moment the handle of the door was softly turned.

A frenzy seized Judy. She was not entirely sure what she was doing, but her hands dabbed at the carpet faster and faster. She was conscious that Clara was with her in the room. She did not look up or say anything. She knew she had one hope and that was the whistle.

Clara came across the room to the end of the bed.

"Saying your prayers? That's a very good idea. You need to. You won't be here to-morrow morning." She leant on the bed-head, her voice rising slightly. "I never wished you any harm, I don't dislike you really, but you've interfered. I knew you were a danger from the day you came to the house. I told you not to stay the moment I knew you'd worked in a hospital. You were a fool not to listen to me."

Judy stretched too far in her search for the whistle and fell over. It was an appalling effort to struggle back on to her hands. It was so much easier to lie on the floor. Clara looked at her almost with sympathy.

"It's no good struggling, you know. They're quite excellent, those sleeping tablets. One is quite a good dose and I dissolved three in boiling water. I think you dislike me. That's queer. I think you'd sympathize if you understood. I won such a good scholarship. I can see myself now, working in bed with the light of a little bit of candle. Propping my books on the pram-rail while I marched the newest baby up and down. Hanging my books above the washtub so that I could learn without touching the pages with my wet fingers. I'll never forget the day when I won that scholarship. When I came home and Mother said, 'You persuade your father to do a decent job of work instead of standing on a box preaching and then you can take it.' Something seemed to snap in my head. I knew my father. Roaring and ranting good-for-nothing. The one good laugh I've ever had was the day I heard they'd shut him up because he thought he was one of the apostles."

Judy's hand touched the whistle. She was groping with such feverish energy that even as she touched it she had moved away again and lost it. A little cry of rage moaned out of her. Clara looked down at her.

"I tell you not to go on struggling. You'll only exhaust yourself. They really are good those sleeping tablets. From that day when I knew I was never to take up my scholarship I swore that one day I'd have a child of my own and that child should live like royalty. It should have everything. More than everything. Money to spend, servants to wait on it. I couldn't hope for a good marriage, so I took Alfred. He was the best I could hope to get. I chose him because of the chemist's shop. A shop's a very nice bit of property, there's something to pass on. The day Desmond was born I looked at him and I said, 'You're not coming into nothing like I did. The shop's doing nicely and every penny it makes will be spent on you'." Her voice cracked. "Then that bomb came."

Judy's little finger touched the whistle. She knew now in what direction it lay. She began to move with more caution. Clara looked at her as if she was a tiresome child.

"Come on, do get into bed. I don't want the trouble of undressing you afterwards. I suppose it might seem natural that you'd fallen on the floor and there'll be a post-mortem anyway, but still, you'll be more comfortable in your bed really. I don't know how long it is before it takes effect, and maybe there's pain; you'd be better lying down." She looked to see if Judy were listening. "Are you listening to me? Get up now and take your things off." Seeing no response she shrugged her shoulders. "Oh, well, there's no hurry. Besides, if you don't mind the floor, I suppose I needn't. I never bothered how Alfred's grandfather went. I hope he suffered. Take my Desmond and shut him up! My Desmond, who's going to be waited on hand and foot! Queer how life turns out. When the old man was dead it came to me all of a flash what I would do. Clear everything out of the house, the dog and the old woman and just keep Aunt Rose. There's Desmond's servant for him; kick her, knock her about, he can do what he likes, no money to pay and we can live here, kept and fed and comfortable until Desmond's eighteen. I dare say she'll have gone naturally by then. It's the right thing to do, you know. Give the children a chance. To be a child without a chance, that's hell. I've been through it and I know. Seems hard, the old people were happy enough, but they'd had their time, so had that smelly old dog. It was right they should go. Queer life is. It's all turning out just as I said it would. My child lacking for nothing, brought up like a prince with somebody to wait on him hand and foot." She looked down at Judy again. "Oh, come on, I can't stand here all night. You poor little fool, what did you want to meddle for? Nobody knows how the old man died. I don't suppose you could do any harm, but I can't risk it."

Judy's little finger was touching the whistle. She moved her hand. Queer how blunt and awkward fingers could become. Why could not they pick the whistle up? She started to mutter. "It's under my hand. Why can't I pick it up? Go on, pick it up. You've got to blow it. I must blow it."

Clara suddenly lost patience. She leant down and caught hold of one of Judy's arms.

"Come on, my girl, get up." She gave her another pull. "Get up and put on your nightdress. What's the point of fighting? If you let yourself go to sleep you won't feel a thing."

Judy, at the touch of Clara's hand, got the necessary strength. Her fingers closed on the whistle, but the effort for the moment overcame her. Once more she rolled on the floor.

Clara held her hypodermic up to the fading fight. It was merely custom that made her do it. She knew that the dose was there. She leant down to have another look at Judy.

"She's out now. I wonder if there would seem anything funny in her being on the floor. It doesn't really matter if there does. They won't find anything wrong." She came round the bed and knelt by Judy's side. "Afraid the needle's a bit blunt, but I couldn't go buying any and the doctor took away the two new ones of the old lady's."

Judy heard what Clara said. She knew what was about to happen. The whistle was in her hand. She knew she must blow it. She made a convulsive movement. Clara held her by the wrist.

"Lie still now. Go to sleep. Nobody wishes you any harm. Just one prick of the needle and off you go."

Judy knew suddenly what she must do. She gave one more convulsive jerk which, for a second, threw Clara's hand off. Then, with a superhuman effort she rolled herself under the bed, and at the same time blew her whistle. It was the last effort she was able to make. Under the bed wave after wave of the mattresses of sleep piled up on top of her, but just as her eyes closed she was conscious that her efforts had been in vain. She felt fingers gripping her wrist.

Judy opened her eyes to find Doctor Mead holding her wrist.

"Well, you've had a fine sleep, young lady. You could do with some lunch now, I should think, couldn't you?"

Judy stared at him.

"I thought I was dead."

Lady Parsons came and sat on the edge of the bed.

"And you very nearly were, dear. If Nick and the police had not got there in time."

"Nick. Where is he?"

Lady Parsons looked at Doctor Mead.

"Do you think we might leave the patient? I know Nick would like a word with her."

Nicholas knelt by Judy's bed.

"Oh, darling, I am an idiot. You see, the police decided to act the moment they heard our story. One of them came up to the place with me just in case you should whistle. When Clara told me you were asleep I damn nearly called up my old cop and burst in. I did watch her take the suit-case upstairs, and if you hadn't answered I'd have knocked her out for six. I am an idiot."

"Where is she?"

"Locked up. I expect she'll be a 'His Majesty's pleasure' affair. We've wired to Bloomfield, he's fetching Desmond to-morrow. Miss Rose is going back with Mother. She can't travel for a day or two. She was pretty upset over the whole thing. My goodness! I could kick myself. If that cop and I hadn't already got that ladder waiting, and if I hadn't legged it up the ladder like a two-year-old when your whistle blew, there'd have been no more Judy."

Judy held out her hand to him.

"Your mother says I'd better tell you that I'm in love with you."

He put his arm round her and drew her to him.

"You don't know about my work, darling. I could be blown to pieces to-morrow. That's not much of a husband, is it?"

"I don't want to seem fussy, but as one who's just missed popping off the world I think you're making rather a fuss about what is merely a possibility. After all, for quite a while yesterday my death was a certainty and it hasn't happened."

Nicholas held her tighter.

"Why didn't I knock that blasted woman on the head? When I think what nearly happened! I am an idiot."

"When I think how precarious life is and how precarious you're making our happiness, then I know you're an idiot."

He drew her to him.

"Really? Then don't let's be idiots any longer. Besides, it's not as though I was marrying an ordinary girl, is it, my little lioness?"

THE END

FURROWED MIDDLEBROW

*titles available in paperback only
**pseudonym of Noel Streatfeild

Printed in Great Britain
by Amazon

39151982R00121